HOPE I

HOPE IN EVERY RAINDROP

Wesley Banks

This is a work of fiction. All of the characters, organizations, and events portrayed in this novel are either products of the author's imagination or are used fictitiously.

Hope In Every Raindrop
Copyright © 2015 by Wesley Banks

First Edition: May 2015

ISBN 978-0-9861934-0-8 (e-book)
ISBN 978-0-9861934-1-5 (paperback)

Chasing Pace Publishing

This book is inspired by my best friend Pace, who I miss with all my heart, and written for Lindsey, a girl that shines more light on this world than she knows.

HOPE IN EVERY RAINDROP

1

KATIE PRICE SET HER LAPTOP on the counter, the cursor still blinking on the blank page as she grabbed a pencil and her hardbound journal. She unlocked the double French doors that led to her back porch and pushed them open wide. The single hook screw groaned in the overhead beam as she settled into her hammock chair. She folded the cover of the journal over on itself and scribbled the date in the top right corner of the first page.

October 29, 2007

Then she did the same thing she had been doing all morning: she stared restlessly at the empty page in front of her.

It had been nearly six months since her father passed away and she'd barely managed to write a single word in that time. It was the longest she'd ever gone without getting something down on the page.

Katie sat there until just before noon, staring out at the Pacific Ocean, the paper and pencil abandoned on her lap. From the back porch she could see almost all seventy miles of the San Diego coastline as it curved slightly towards Mexico around the Baja Peninsula.

The combination of the waves gently crashing on the beach and the slow sway of her hammock stilled her thoughts. Normally she would have reveled in the quiet, but she was restless and wanted more than anything to find her next story.

She pressed the lead tip of the pencil against the paper, hoping for that one word that would send her off into endless hours of writing. Nothing came except the interrupting chirp of her phone.

She eased herself out of the chair and set the pencil and journal on the counter next to her computer as she walked back inside. The screen on her phone lit up with a number that was all too familiar: her agent.

For a moment, she held the phone in her hand, thinking she might just slide the ringer to silent and take a walk on the beach. Or better yet, she could throw the phone on the ground and stomp on it until it shattered into a thousand tiny pieces. Unfortunately, she knew that wouldn't solve her problems. Not answering would just mean within a few hours her agent would pull into the driveway in her fancy BMW—if not today, then tomorrow or the next day. Katie didn't have any options.

"Hello, Samantha," Katie said, drawing out her full name in annoyance.

"Please tell me you've got something."

Katie half-heartedly tried to lie. "I've got something, Sam."

"Oh, Katie," Sam said. "What am I going to do with you? You can't even lie well lately. At least embellish a little, make up the name of your next lead character or hint at some masterful plot you're still working out the details on."

Katie didn't respond.

"Still not writing, I take it?"

Katie let out a brief sigh as she stared back out towards the water. "Not a word."

"Katie, you know I love you. You're my little prodigy. And while I know you're only twenty-one, you're playing in the big leagues now. Your publisher is breathing down my neck— if you don't come up with something in the next month, they're going to start requesting you return a portion, if not all, of the advance for this next book. I'll keep trying to cover for you, but with the economy the way it is…well, you know.

Again Katie didn't say anything. She just nodded to herself, as if Sam were standing right in front of her with her fancy high heels and matching designer purse. Her agent's career had taken off after Katie's first couple of novels had made Katie the youngest woman on record with back-to-back bestsellers in the same calendar year.

"I don't mean to pry, but have you tried perhaps reading through some of your father's old work, to see if that might spark something?"

Katie reached down and picked up a dark brown book with a title scrawled in gold letters. It was her father's first anthology of poems—the first literary work ever published under his name. It had never gained much traction with the public, but the poems had long been one of the reasons Katie had become a writer. His words always filled her with hope, and she had wanted so badly to pass that same feeling on to others.

She ran her hands over the lettering of her father's name on the spine of the book. Over the past few months she must have read each poem ten times, especially one he wrote for her.

> *Let the rain add to our tears*
> *Until the day when all the pain has stopped*
> *And we will say there was hope in every raindrop*

To this day Katie would swear that her father was twice, even three times, the writer she was, but as a poet he never managed to find the success she had in fiction.

"I haven't, but maybe I'll try," Katie lied, this time convincingly.

"I think you should. I think that may help you find your voice again."

Katie walked towards the bookshelf behind her couch and started to speak again, but Sam cut her off. "I'm sorry, hon, but I've got another call coming in that I have to take. I'll touch base with you in a week or so. We need to at least give them a sample to keep 'em busy. Remember, thirty days."

And with that Sam hung up.

Katie set her phone on the end table and pressed her father's book back in its place on the shelf.

"How did I ever write a *New York Times* Best Seller?" she said out loud. Her own books stared back at her. The stories had always come so easily before.

She turned to go back to the porch, forgetting about the boxes of her father's stuff she had stacked behind the couch.

As she moved, she stubbed her toe on the corner of one box and knocked over another that was next to it.

"Shoot," she said to herself as she reached down towards her foot.

When she stood, she realized that half the contents from the box she'd hit had spilled out across the floor. She knelt, starting to put them back in the box labeled "Dad's Stuff." Most of the contents were old journals or notes her father had made while drafting his books, and it didn't take her long to toss everything back where it belonged. But, one object had slid about ten feet across the room.

It was a small wooden container that looked to be about the size of a cigar box. There was a metal clasp on the front that held it shut and two hinges on the back that split it in two perfect halves. Nothing about the container looked familiar. In fact, Katie was pretty sure she had never seen it before.

A shiver ran through her body and tears formed in her eyes as she unclasped the lock and opened it. Sitting on top was a small cross—actually, just two sticks tied together with twine. But underneath that cross was a photo of her mother. It was a small faded portrait, maybe two inches by three inches. The corners of the picture had started to peel away and the glossy surface was beginning to crack.

She had seen this picture before, but not for a very long time. Not since she had finished her first novel.

Katie put the photo back down next to the cross and lifted out a gold-plated pocket watch with the name *Price* inscribed on the back. She didn't have to close her eyes to perfectly recall her father incessantly checking the watch and stuffing it back in his tweed jacket whenever he was stuck in his writing.

Below the watch, however, was an object she was sure she had not seen before.

Katie turned the folded piece of paper over in her hand. It wasn't normal lined paper. It had a familiar feel to it, except for the small bulge in the center. One side was taped to prevent it from unfolding. She used her thumbnail to gently peel back the tape.

As she opened it, she realized why it seemed familiar, though she was certain she had never seen this specific one. It was a map of the United States.

Katie pushed aside several boxes and cleared an area large enough to lay out the entire map flat on her wood floor. There were several pin-sized holes scattered across the surface. In the lower right corner, just above the legend, she found a dart held down by another piece of tape.

She removed the dart and set it aside, revealing several words written in cursive below it.

The ink was slightly faded, but she could still make out each word.

> *There are stories all around you if you only take the time to look.*
>
> *Love always,*
>
> *Katherine*

Katie felt her body tremble again as tears streamed slowly down her cheeks and onto the map. She quickly ran her hands under her eyes, wiping away the tears, and tried to blot out the wet spots on the paper with the hem of her shirt.

Her mother must have given this to her father before she was even born.

For a moment, Katie just stared at the beautiful handwritten words from her mother. Her eyes traced the sweeping arc of each letter as it ran into the next. She repeated the words again in her head, but her emotions clouded their specific meaning.

Her thoughts trailed off as her gaze returned to the silver dart lying next to her. The tip was sharp and the body was rough as she ran her hand over it towards the three blue fins at the other end.

Then, it all dawned on her.

Katie quickly grabbed the map and trotted to the kitchen, ignoring the pain in her stubbed toe. Opening a drawer, she grabbed a roll of scotch tape and walked out to her porch.

She turned to face the house, looking for a section of the wall large enough to hang the map. There was just enough room between two of the back windows. She taped the four corners, pressing the paper as close to the wall as possible.

She took several steps back with the dart in her right hand, imagining her father doing something similar all those years ago. But as she looked back at the map, something seemed wrong. She could make out the name of each state and in many cases some of the cities that were printed in larger letters. Walking back over, she ran her hand across several places where she saw holes. Instead of feeling a smooth surface, she felt the punctured paper pressing out towards her. The dart couldn't have been thrown at the map facing this direction.

She set the dart on the handrail and removed the tape she had just placed on each of the corners. Then, she turned it over so the blank side faced her and again ran her fingers over the myriad of pin holes. Smooth.

Standing back at the edge of her porch, all she could see was a plain white piece of paper taped to her wall. Still, she could aim towards the center of the map and hit Missouri,

Nebraska, or Kansas. Or for the corners and land on Florida, Georgia, New York, Maine, Washington, California, and so on. So, she picked up the dart and turned her back to the map. Counting to three, she spun back around and let the dart go without hesitation. It wasn't a perfect throw, but it stuck solidly to the wall with a thud.

She pulled the dart from the wall, careful to reach around to the front of the map with one hand and mark the spot as she turned it over and set it on the porch floor. The small hole was in the dead center of a city she had never heard of in South Carolina.

The first drop of afternoon showers landed on the steps a few feet from her. Looking out again into the vastness of the deep blue rolling waves, Katie couldn't help but feel excitement at the simple thought of one word.

Bishopville.

2

THE FIRST DROP OF RAIN landed square on the toe of his boot. The second drop hit the back of his hand, which was wrapped around the handle of an old wooden claw hammer. He drove one more nail into the post, then twisted the hammer upwards and bent the head of the nail back over itself. He gave a quick tug on the hog wire to make sure the nail would hold it tight to the post. It held firm.

Kyle Walker stood up and looked back at his work over the past few weeks as he removed his cap and ran his arm across his forehead, wiping away the sweat. There were only three more rows of posts to dig and several rolls of fence to hang before the new runs would be finished.

He thought about it for a moment, running a few quick calculations in his head. It would take him five days to finish, maybe four if Doc lent a hand for a day or two. It felt good to be so close to done, and finally getting the dogs out of the barn.

A few more drops of rain fell across the brim of his hat as he looked west towards the Blue Ridge Mountains. King was nowhere in sight, but that was expected with a storm moving in.

He walked the hammer and bag of nails back over to a small work bench and turned to stand underneath the large pine lintel that spanned the barn door. Leaning against the door, he crossed his right boot over his left leg. Small chips of red paint crumbled onto his right shoulder as he shifted slightly, his eyes scanning the horizon.

He looked down across the inner coastal plains of South Carolina. It was a land of gently rolling hills and forests cut through by slow-moving rivers heading to the Atlantic Ocean. An outer belt of longleaf pines that most people knew as the "Flatwoods" stood between him and the western sand hills. Live oaks, cypress trees, and dense shrubs of hollies and wax myrtle filled in most of the land. Above all, Kyle loved the open savanna—the smooth cordgrass that lined the outskirts of the wetlands to the east and the thick patches of wiregrass that covered the endless fields.

He closed his eyes and let the western winds blow against his face. Seconds later, the world changed around him. The still pines in the distance began to bend slightly in the wind, shaking loose several pine cones and littering them across the ground. The darkness that had seemed miles away suddenly surrounded him. A flash of lightning struck. The sky opened up and heavy drops of rain fell, as if someone had turned over a thousand buckets all at once.

From several feet behind him two of the dogs began to howl at the storm, and several others let out guttural growls. But for the most part they sat silently and watched, looking in the same direction that Kyle did.

Kyle looked intently at the empty distance, his eyes darting from the tree line to the open fields.

One thousand objects per second. Myelinated nerves can fire up to one thousand times per second in the human body and transmit information at two hundred miles per hour, making the human eye one of the body's most complex organs. Or so he had once read.

As King came into sight, none of that mattered. Science could measure speed, reaction time, or how many neurons fired when a human being processed an image. But as he watched King run, shifting slightly left or right, it seemed as if the rain wasn't even fast enough to touch him. And there was no science to explain that.

King disappeared behind a thick line of brush, but as Kyle's eyes moved to the other side where the dog should have reappeared, he was nowhere to be found.

Another minute went by before Kyle looked down, smiling at King sitting silently next to him.

3

TWO THOUSAND, FOUR HUNDRED, and seven miles. Through Arizona, New Mexico, Texas, Louisiana, Mississippi, Alabama, and Georgia. That was the route from San Diego, California to Bishopville, South Carolina. It took Katie just over four days.

The entire trip, she couldn't concentrate on anything but her father.

Is this how he found inspiration? Did he plan his trips? Was Mom always with him?

Hundreds of questions continued to race through her head. She had resolved to do no prior research about Bishopville for fear she might convince herself not to go; once the dart had left her hand, she'd known her fate was sealed. This is what her father would have done. She was scared. She was nervous. She was determined. But most of all, she was…hungry. Her stomach growled.

It was Monday morning—11:03 a.m. Pacific Standard Time, to be exact. Which meant it was 2:03 p.m. where she currently was on the East Coast, and she hadn't eaten anything since the night before.

As she drove through the small town, she wasn't quite sure which direction to go. She looked up at the Garmin GPS that hung just below her rearview mirror. *Recalculating.* She flicked the screen a couple times, but the map didn't update. It had stopped working about ten minutes ago, when she'd passed the *Bishopville Town Limits* sign. She'd left California with no plans of what to do upon arriving in South Carolina.

She passed a Texaco station on her left, where two black men sat outside the store in lawn chairs. After that, she didn't see anything but farmland and forest for several miles. Katie was about to pull over and attempt to get some type of signal with her phone to locate a nearby restaurant when she saw a small wooden structure a few hundred feet ahead.

It looked like a convenience store from the 1950s. There was a porch out front, similar to the kind she'd seen on Cracker Barrel storefronts, and a sign above the overhang that read "Pearl's Place." Two cars were parked out front in the dirt lot, and it looked like as good a place as any to stop. If they didn't have any food, at least she could ask for directions.

The inside of the store was absolutely storybook, and Katie couldn't help but smile after a few steps through the front door. She paused and let the writer in her take over, going through everything in as much detail as possible.

To her left was a glass counter with wood trim that extended all the way to the back of the store. She didn't see anyone behind the counter or near the cash register, which appeared to be an antique. As she stepped closer, she couldn't help but think it looked similar to the old-fashioned typewriter that her father had used—though instead of a metal body with plastic keys, the cash register was made of fine wood with different inlay patterns. The numbers and symbols were inset in brass, bronze, copper, and other flat metals with fancy enamel designs.

On shelves behind the counter sat boxes, bags, and bottles of all the typical home goods: flour, salt, sugar, and a myriad of other indispensable products.

She took a few more steps into the store and discovered a refrigerated section in the back. It was small, but it had the essentials like bacon, eggs, cheese, and milk, along with a multitude of meats that looked freshly cut and wrapped.

The middle of the store was full of rows of breads, potato chips, granola bars, and smelled faintly of pure vanilla. One row was clearly marked "Local Goods," and contained what appeared to be homemade jams or jellies, in particular several different variations of peach.

As she walked around the store, she used her phone to snap some photos of anything she thought she could use to write about later: brand names she had never heard of, how certain foods were packaged and stacked on the shelves, old pictures and signs that hung from the walls. She also took some quick notes with the pad she carried in her purse, but soon all that took a backseat to her growling stomach.

A door that led to the back opened and an older man in a white apron and black wire-rim glasses emerged. He was bald except for a short row of hair resting about an inch above each ear, and a bushy white mustache neatly cropped under his nose. Katie couldn't help but think he looked just like the Monopoly man.

The man seemed a bit taken aback when he saw a young woman standing in front of him. He adjusted his glasses as if he might be seeing things and then said, "May, uh, I, uh, help you, Miss?"

Katie smiled and her stomach growled again. "Actually yes, I was just looking for a place to..."

"Eat," the old man said, finishing her sentence. "I may be old, but I'm not deaf," he added at the confusion on Katie's face.

"Is there a..."

The old man again finished her sentence, "restaurant in town? Well, yes and no. We've got food here, but I wouldn't say we're a restaurant. Though I could whip you up a pretty mean sandwich."

Before Katie could respond he took a few more steps forward, wiped his hand on his apron, and extended it towards her. "I'm Earl, and you are..."

"Katie," she said, finishing his sentence for a change.

He chuckled to himself and turned to walk further into the store.

There weren't many options on the menu at Pearl's Place, but the ham and cheese sandwich that Earl made was absolutely amazing. An inside-out ham and cheese sandwich—that's what Earl had called it. His secret? Butter each slice of bread and sprinkle the outside with parmesan cheese. So simple, but so delicious. Either that or Katie was just so famished that anything would have been amazing.

"I hope Earl here isn't bothering you," a woman said from somewhere behind Katie.

Katie turned on her stool at the only high-top table in the store, to find a plump gray-haired woman holding a large push broom. Her cheeks puffed into little round cotton balls as she smiled, and her voice had that endearing quality of a wise grandmother.

Katie wiped a drop of mustard from her lip and swallowed the last bit of her sandwich. "Not at all."

"Not at all," Earl quickly added. "Miss Price here is a famous writer!" Earl added, which he had learned through the endless conversation he'd engaged her in while making the sandwich.

The woman ignored Earl and instead introduced herself. "Excuse his manners, he's all shy at first, but once you get him talking he just doesn't know when to stop. I'm Pearl."

"Katie."

"Well, Katie, it is a pleasure to meet you."

"I love your store," Katie blurted out.

"Thank you, dear, but I'm afraid it's not much these days," Pearl said, looking towards the worn wooden beams that framed the ceiling.

"Miss Price is looking for a story!" Earl interrupted again excitedly.

"Oh, Earl, would you hush up and stop bothering this poor woman." Pearl turned back and whispered to Katie, "I'm sorry, dear, he's always like this when we get somebody in the store."

"It's okay," Katie said. "I actually am looking for a story to tell."

Earl's smile was ear to ear as he looked at Pearl with smug satisfaction. "See?"

"Hmm. Well, I'm afraid Bishopville isn't exactly a big story town," Pearl said, ignoring her husband. "Not a lot goes on around here. I s'pose that's why most people stick around."

Katie's smile faded a bit at the news, but she resolved herself as she recalled the words that started her on this journey in the first place.

There are stories all around you if you only take the time to look.

"Anyways, enjoy your lunch, dear. C'mon Earl, let's leave Miss Price to finish her meal in peace."

"But she already finished her sandwich," Earl pleaded.

Pearl just glared at him, and Earl stepped from behind the counter and followed her towards the front of the store. She handed him the broom and he began to sweep the floors between each row of shelves.

Katie crumpled up the wax paper she had been using for a plate, quickly ate the dill pickle wedge that Earl had given her, and found Pearl tidying up behind the register.

"How much for the sandwich and drink?"

"That will be five dollars even," Pearl said with a great big smile.

Katie pulled out her pocketbook and was about to hand over a credit card when she thought better of it. Instead, she pulled out a ten dollar bill and slid it across the counter. "I don't need any change," she added politely.

Earl was still sweeping the floors and grumbling to himself. "You should tell her about the dogs," he kept mumbling. "I bet she'd like to know about the dogs. And Kyle," he added.

"She don't want to hear about no silly dogs," Pearl shouted back.

Katie couldn't help her curiosity. "What dogs?"

Pearl sighed and tapped her finger on the countertop as she looked at Katie, a reserved look on her face. "Miss Price, I just don't think you ought to be chasin' after rumors is all."

"What rumors?"

Pearl carried on, talking more in thought than complete sentences. "Doc just hasn't been the same since…I mean, he

17

still practices an' all, but…and…Kyle. He really has grown up to be a fine young man, but he's just gotten so attached to them dogs." She paused, taking in a deep breath as she fiddled with the white huck rag in her hands. "I just don't think they're the type of people that want strangers snoopin' around their business. No offense, dear."

"None taken. Sometimes us writers have to do a little bit of snoopin', though. What were you saying about the dogs?"

Pearl hesitated again, but after a few seconds gave in. "Well, I haven't seen it with my own eyes."

"I have." Earl added.

"Hush up. You haven't either."

"Seen what?"

"Supposedly certain people come to town just to see these dogs."

"They do, I've seen 'em," Earl added again.

Pearl just glared at him until he walked a few feet away and went back to sweeping the floors.

"Like I was saying: people from all over come to see these dogs."

"Why? What's so special about the dogs?"

"To be honest, dear, I'm not sure. I'm not much of an animal person myself. 'Cept the ones we keep around to butcher and sell."

Earl couldn't help it. He was like a cat waiting for just the right time to pounce. He walked briskly up to Katie. "They're race dogs. But not just any ol' race dogs. They're the cream o' the crop. The cat's meow. The bee's knees. The best thing since little apples. You can't beat 'em." He looked up at Katie, who was listening intently, and went on. "Mainly 'cause they're part wolf. Got them long lean legs that can outrun

18

anythin'. But 'specially 'cause they're Carolina dogs," he said with a prideful grin.

"Earl, you don't know that."

"I do so. Seen it with my own eyes. Seen the boy out runnin' with 'em.

Pearl just shook her head. "It snows here 'bout twice a year. That doesn't even make sense."

"You don't happen to have an address, do you?" Katie asked excitedly, drawing a somewhat surprised look from Pearl.

"I don't. But..." Pearl paused, reaching under the counter for a pencil and a scrap piece of paper. She jotted down directions quickly, the loose skin between her elbow and shoulder jiggling as she wrote, and handed the paper to Katie.

"I hope you find whatever you're looking for, dear."

"Thanks. I hope I do, too," Katie said.

"Oh you'll find it if you look hard 'nough. There's somethin' magical 'bout them dogs," Earl said, drawing a final stare from his wife that caused him to shuffle to the other end of the store as the front door closed behind Katie.

4

ALMOST AN HOUR LATER, Katie pulled to a stop in front of a dirt road that was split in half by a large banyan tree. The tree's roots had taken over the driveway and protruded from the orange and brown dirt like natural speed bumps. She hadn't driven more than a few miles since she left Pearl's Place, but the roads were long and empty. Pole-mounted street signs were missing or supplanted by barely legible makeshift boards.

Katie looked back at the directions Pearl had jotted down.

Drive straight down Anderson until you see a slight bend in the road.

Take a left onto a dirt road. House will be on the left.

"Nothing ventured, nothing gained." Katie said to herself as she took a deep breath and made a left turn.

The sand and dirt crunched under the tires of Katie's light blue convertible as it turned off the asphalt road. She was too busy looking ahead to see the small cloud of dust kick up from the tires as she eased to a stop several hundred yards later.

On her left was a faded white double-wide trailer with a long front porch. The roof was dark green, and matched the leaves of several tall trees that stood behind the house.

She put the car in park and pressed the ignition button adjacent to the steering wheel. The lights on the dash went off and she stepped out of the car.

Directly across from the house was a two-story barn. One of the oversized sliding doors was pulled open, but the sun cast a shadow that prevented Katie from seeing farther than a few feet into the barn.

She took several steps up the front porch. As Katie extended her hand to knock on the screen door, a man asked from the side of the porch, "May I help you?"

Startled, Katie pulled her hand back and cleared her throat, but before she spoke she was taken aback at the sheer size of the man standing there. Perhaps a few inches over six feet, his legs were like tree trunks tight against his jeans, and his forearms looked more like calves as he wrapped his hand around a large walking staff that stopped just past his shoulders. He had a neatly trimmed thin white beard and his hair was pulled back in a ponytail that hung barely above his shoulders.

Every facet of him seemed imposing. Until he smiled.

His cheeks puffed with a light red hue and there was nothing but kindness in his eyes. It was like looking at a fitter version of Santa Claus.

"I'm looking for Doctor Anderson," she finally managed.

The stranger made his way around the porch railing and took the steps two at a time until he was standing right in front of her.

"Well, last time I checked that was still me," he said as he held out his hand. "But you can call me Doc. And you are..."

"Oh, excuse me. I'm Katie Price." As she extended her hand, her elbow brushed against the small spiral notepad poking from her purse.

"I was actually going to say reporter," Doc said. He hesitated. "But...a reporter wouldn't be out here in a sundress and designer boots. At least not a reporter who's done her homework. And you don't seem like a reporter, anyways."

He glanced back at her car parked on the dirt path. "And I don't believe you're here as a buyer, or prospective buyer anyways. For one, the pups are only six weeks old, and for two we haven't told anyone about them just yet. Not to mention one of them would likely ruin your nice car."

Katie was about to speak, but Doc stopped her by holding up his hand. "Wait, don't tell me." He rubbed his thumb and index finger against his chin. "No, I think I was nearly right the first time. So, if not a reporter then...a writer?"

"How did you do that?"

"I apologize, it's an old habit of mine. I really should have seen it sooner." He motioned to the notepad sticking out of her purse, and then back to the car. "It was obvious that you're some type of writer, and last I checked reporters don't make enough money for fancy cars. Of course, neither do most writers. Unless they're very good writers, that is. So," Doc continued, "what brings a young writer all the way out here?"

Before Katie could respond, she saw something move out of the corner of her eye. She turned to see a black and white piebald dog with shaggy hair trotting away from five puppies chasing furiously after her.

Doc laughed softly to himself. "She's tired of nursing."

Katie was still a bit confused until the dog was only a few steps from the porch. Up close, it was clear to see her stomach was loose and sagging, as if she'd been nursing for days on end.

Doc walked past Katie and down the steps. "Excuse me one moment?"

Katie nodded.

"Come on, Biscuit," Doc said, tapping the dog lightly on the back of her neck. "I've got just the hiding spot for you."

Biscuit followed Doc around the side of the house. Katie was left alone on the porch with five wild puppies still running in her direction.

When they reached the steps, the pups looked up at her and began to whine. At first Katie didn't understand, then one of them put his paws on the bottom step and tried to make his way up. They were still too young to make it over the steps, which were a few inches higher than they were tall.

Katie walked down and sat on the bottom step.

Four of the puppies were black with a small white triangular marking on their chest and spots of white on their feet, but one of them was entirely black. They nuzzled against her legs, tracking little dirt prints over the toe of her leather boots. She reached down and picked the solid black one up and held it in front of her, one hand on each side of the puppy and her thumbs wrapped under his front legs.

Katie pulled him close to her and ran her fingers over his fuzzy body. The puppy looked up at her and wrinkled its nose slightly, sniffing at the air around him.

In a higher-than-normal pitch Katie looked down at the dog and said, "What do you smell?" She scratched his head and around his small ears, already pricked straight up. "I bet the smell of my clothes and perfume is all brand new to you, huh?"

As she spoke, the puppy suddenly started to scramble out of her lap at the same time the others scurried below the steps in front of her.

"And where do you think you all are going?"

She knelt forward off the steps, adjusting her dress so her knees pressed into the grass. She was about to look down under the porch when she heard a low growl a few feet to her left. She hadn't seen or heard a single thing except the puppies, but now a large black dog stood several yards away.

Katie drew in her breath quickly, but didn't move.

His head was huge relative to his body and was lowered, so it was even with his tail. His teeth were not bared, but he was definitely making some sort of growling noise as he stared directly at her. From her knees the dog was almost eye level. She noticed there was no collar around the dog's neck, unlike Biscuit. And a defined strip of fur down the dog's back bristled.

She wasn't sure if she should back slowly up the steps to the porch, make a run for her car, or just sit there on all fours and not move until Doc returned.

Before she could make a decision, a man appeared on the dirt and grass path several hundred feet behind the dog. With the sun at his back she could only see his silhouette, but he appeared to be holding something up to his mouth. From where she was it looked exactly like a person standing with a harmonica—but not quite a harmonica. Something else.

A high-pitched whistle lifted over the breeze and ran down towards her. The black dog growled once more, turned, and ran. His gait was smooth and effortless. With long fluid strides his back remained perfectly flat as he moved across the land. When Katie finally took her eyes off the dog and looked back towards where the man had been standing, she saw nothing. A few seconds later, the dog crested the horizon and both of them were gone.

Katie stood and brushed her knees off as Doc approached from the barn.

"Sorry about that," he said. "But I've got Biscuit a nice little hiding spot in one of the new runs. She should be safe for a few hours at least. So...you were in the middle of telling me why you're here."

"Well, I'm here to write."

"Ah, yes, a writer who likes to write. Quite ambitious of you," he said with a slight grin as he walked back over to one of two empty rocking chairs and sat down. "May I ask how exactly you ended up here, though? I mean, there are so many places in the world to visit. I dare say Bishopville, South Carolina wasn't at the top of your list. I would have guessed some place fancy like New York City or San Francisco."

Katie didn't hesitate. She had thought about this question for a long time during her drive from California. Was what she was doing silly? Just because this was the way her father found his inspiration didn't mean it would work for her. But around a thousand miles into this trip, she had remembered a story her father once told her.

"In 1937," she began aloud, relating the story to Doc, "horse racing was one of the most popular sports in the United States. So popular, that to this day people could probably tell you stories about a famous leviathan of a horse named War Admiral. After winning the Triple Crown that year, War Admiral will always be remembered as one of the greatest race horses to live.

"But something else happened in 1937 that almost nobody knows. Another horse, competing mostly in smaller races on the West Coast, actually took home more prize money that year than any other horse. Running in these small races, this horse began to stir hope in the hearts of Americans at a time when the Great Depression had hit hard and hope was scarce.

"A year later, the horse's owner traveled East demanding a match race between the overpowering War Admiral and the no-name filly from the West."

"You are talking about the horse called Seabiscuit, are you not?" Doc said.

"I am. But, my question to you is: in which town did the story of Seabiscuit begin?"

Doc's eyes lit with excitement as his grin stretched across his face. "I see your point very clearly, young lady."

"Small towns often have big stories," she said.

"That was a lovely answer, but not to my question. I meant, how exactly did you end up *here*?"

Katie thought about it a moment and said, "I more or less just pointed to a place on the map and drove."

"Now that is an even better answer," he said.

As Doc rocked back in his chair, Katie noticed a small butterfly that floated softly around the faded porch rail until it found a spot to rest next to a deep knot in the wood. Katie looked back towards Doc. His eyes were also fixed on the yellow and black striped wings.

"Would it be intruding if I was to take a look around the place?" Katie asked. "I'd really love to just find a place to sit and maybe jot down a few notes before it gets dark. Maybe even see the rest of the dogs?"

Doc didn't respond. He was looking at Katie, but he didn't seem to see her. After a brief moment, he nodded. "Well now, let me see. Today is Saturday, yesterday was Friday, and tomorrow is Sunday. Yep, looks like I'm free, Miss Hannah."

Katie brushed a tendril of brown hair from her face and tucked it behind her ear. She blushed a little, thinking he'd forgotten her name already.

"You mean Katie?"

"Of course I meant Katie!" he laughed.

He stood up and extended his arm like a father about to walk his daughter down the aisle. "I would like to think I could give you a proper tour of the place. That is, if you have the time."

"I have all the time in the world," she said.

But the truth was, she now had less than three weeks.

5

"WELL LET ME JUST CHECK one thing inside and we'll be on our way."

"Actually, do you have some place I could change real quick?" Katie said. She held the fabric of her dress away from her skin and shrugged.

"I do, and that would probably be a good decision."

Katie walked back to her car and pushed the suitcase in the backseat onto its side. She unzipped the main compartment and pulled out a pair of jeans that were sitting on top, and dug around until she found a dark green pullover.

Doc was still holding the screen door open when she walked back up the stairs. "Just to the left there, through the kitchen. I'll be out here when you're ready."

"Thanks," Katie said.

The bathroom felt tiny as Katie closed the door behind her. It was just a half bath with a small mirror over the sink. She wasn't quite sure what to expect, but to her surprise it was clean. Actually, it was spotless.

She looked into the mirror. Her hair was all frizzy, her eyes had small bags under them, and her lips looked as dry as the deserts she'd driven through in Arizona.

Katie crossed both of her arms and lifted her dress over her head. *Why did I pack a dress?* She folded it up and set it on her purse. She turned the faucet on and lightly splashed some water over her face. Immediately she felt better.

She ran her hands through her hair and pulled it up into a ponytail, and ran some chap stick over her lips. After her jeans and sweater were on she looked back in the mirror.

For a moment she paused. Her smile faded and she just looked back at the girl in the mirror. This is crazy, she thought. She suddenly felt out of her element. How did her father ever do adventurous things like this?

Sam's words came back to her. *You're in the big leagues now.*

Katie let out a deep breath, grabbed her dress, and shoved a few things back in her purse.

When she walked outside Doc was sitting back in his rocking chair. She walked over and tossed the dress in the front seat of the car, which slid off the shiny leather and onto the floor next to her sandals. "Okay, I'm ready," she said with a smile.

It was midafternoon when Katie and Doc left. They had walked for what felt like hours, but the sun still hung high against the clouds. All that time spent sitting at her beach house in San Diego for the last six months was starting to show. Her feet hurt, her calves hurt...even her shoulders hurt from just carrying around her purse for so long.

Katie had tried to jot down notes as she followed behind Doc, but it proved to be too much. She was overwhelmed by the enormity of his property, and the nonstop information he had to offer. Instead, she just tried to take it all in.

Whenever you can't write the story, become the story. Or so her father used to say.

Doc's property was just over one thousand acres. To put that into perspective, the whole town of Bishopville itself was only five square miles, or three thousand acres. Doc owned one-third of that.

He had divided the property into four sections, and he introduced each one as such: the barn, the junkyard, the farm, and the land.

First up was the barn, which was just a short stroll across the dirt path in front of the house.

"This is it," he said with a smile, his cheeks rolling into little balls that forced his eyes to squint.

The stalls looked empty except for bits of hay scattered about. Several harnesses, leashes, and other miscellaneous ropes and cords hung from the wall. Just inside the doors was a wooden bench with several tool boxes arranged in a neat row. It was probably the cleanest barn Katie had ever seen. Okay, it was the only barn she had ever seen.

"Is this where you keep the dogs?" Katie asked.

"It is, when they aren't training."

Katie continued to look around.

"Come," Doc said. "There are a lot more exciting things than this."

It was just around the left side of the house and a few hundred yards past a copse of pine trees before they reached what Doc referred to as the junkyard. Katie expected to see, well, a junkyard. They obviously didn't have garbage men out here, so she figured maybe that's what they did in these small towns. That couldn't have been further from the truth.

As they approached, Katie was absorbed with the different trees and colors that still lingered in late fall. She almost didn't even see the sixty or so trailer homes in the middle of a small field, situated in three neatly stacked rows. Some were propped up on huge cinder blocks, while others looked as if they had sunk into the ground after sitting there for so long.

"I used to rent 'em, back in the day," Doc proclaimed. "Problem was about twenty years ago people didn't want trailer homes no more. They wanted the real thing, and it just didn't feel right not to buy them back. So, here they are."

"What are you going to do with them?"

"Well, actually, I don't really have any plans. They've trickled back in over the years and I imagine they'll sit there until they eventually rust away."

Katie wanted to object. She wanted to tell him he could scrap them, or disassemble them for parts. But when she saw the way he looked at them, it was almost as if he had some weird sense of pride. Like this was his hobby. His collection. Most people don't collect trailer homes, but who was she to judge?

As Katie followed Doc to their next stop she noticed the grass was unkept, and debris from the trailer homes was littered about for what seemed like several hundred feet. She stepped over the occasional tire or hitch, and even a few windows and doors.

When they approached the farm Doc shouted out a warning, pointing to several flattened areas of grass. "Watch your step. Lots of hogs been rootin' around through here."

Doc's advice, as prudent as it was, came a little too late.

Not more than a few steps in, Katie stepped on a somewhat crunchy, somewhat creamy substance.

"That'd be hog scat, Miss Price," Doc said, turning to face her. "Pig poop," he clarified. He squatted down next to several tracks and pointed into the distance. "And by the looks of it, they went that way."

"How can you tell?"

"Hogs' hooves are rounded in the back and pointed towards the front, making it easy to tell which way a hog is travelling. And, well, I can see them over there."

Katie couldn't help but laugh when she looked to her left. Sure enough, there were five hogs just standing there staring right back at her. As Katie stood up, one of them took several steps forward and snorted.

"They're not dangerous. Right?"

Doc chuckled as he continued on. "I s'pose that depends on the day."

They continued on their way through a narrow path cut in the woods and about ten minutes later, arrived at the farm.

When people talked about farms or farming, Katie always found it hard not to imagine old men in overalls sifting through fields of corn, stopping every now and then to grab hold of an ear of corn and proclaim in the most hillbilly accent possible, "Now dat dere is a fine lookin' vegetable." What lay in front of her, though, was nothing of the sort.

Tobacco, cotton, soybeans, corn, hay, wheat, peaches, apples, and peanuts—those were the types of crops she expected to see. Doc did not grow any of those.

Instead, for as far as Katie could see, there were row upon row of giant sunflowers.

"Do you know how sunflowers got their name?" Doc said as he walked towards them. He was over six feet tall, but when he went to touch the soft yellow petal, he still had to reach up over his head.

"Their scientific name is Helianthus, but that's actually a combination of two words. Helios, the Greek word for sun, and Anthos, the Greek word for flower."

Katie continued walking. Just a few steps past Doc, a trail opened up amongst the flowers. As she stepped in between the thousands of flowers, her thoughts rushed through her parted lips like a soft breeze. "They're beautiful."

She looked closer, from one flower to another. They looked identical, but it wasn't their similar color, height, or size that caught her attention. It was their orientation. Every single flower was pointed in the same direction.

Doc continued walking through the manmade trail, giant sunflowers flanking both sides, as Katie followed slowly behind.

"Did you ever notice that they all face the same direction?" she asked from several feet behind him.

Doc stopped momentarily and pulled the bandana from around his neck to wipe the sweat from his forehead. Then he folded it back into a triangle and tied it around his neck once more.

Katie took out her phone as Doc stood in the middle of the worn path, hands stacked atop one another, leaning against his walking stick, thousands of giant sunflowers looking over his shoulder. She quickly took several pictures of him as he began to speak.

"From sunrise to sunset, she follows her love
Making sure not to take her eyes off him

Not even for a second time,

Perennially in love with her love'"

Katie had spent countless nights with her father, listening to writers recite their poems in bookstores, libraries, cafes, or bars. As she looked at Doc, she recalled her father's words.

The good poets, they'll look out towards their audience to make eye contact and entwine them into the story. The great poets...they'll look back to the memory where these words began and forget the audience altogether.

Doc's voice was deep like the still waters of an empty ocean, and he gazed into the distance like he was searching for someone or something.

Katie broke the momentary silence. "Who wrote that?"

"To be honest, I'm not quite sure. My wife used to recite those words when we walked through here. There was more from the myth, but alas, I'm old and have forgotten most of them. We best be goin' though, gonna be late."

"Late for what?"

Doc didn't answer, he just turned back around and started walking down the trail, and Katie followed.

When the rows of sunflowers finally ended another trail began, lined with smooth cordgrass on either side.

Along the way, Doc continued to point out each and every plant and flower, first in their Latin name, and then in their more informal common name. *Pinus palustris*, the longleaf pine. *Asclepias tuberosa*, better known as the butterfly weed. *Enemion*, the false rue anomena. *Aesculus parviflora*, bottlebrush buckeye. The list was never ending.

The more Doc spoke, the more Katie's mind wandered back to Earl's last words: *There's somethin' magical 'bout them dogs.*

It wasn't the words themselves that had captured her attention, nor the way Earl had said them. Rather it was the look in his eyes—as if he had seen something. Something secret and wonderful. But what?

Her mind raced with possibilities. She loved the idea of something magical for her story. Katie was so caught up in her thoughts that she almost ran right into Doc as he stopped next to an enormous oak tree.

He stretched his legs out as he leaned against the tree, his body fitting just barely between two roots protruding from the ground. He had spent the last two hours dragging Katie here and there, sharing all the tidbits of information about the property. It seemed as though he had a story for everything. And while Katie had enjoyed most of it, she wanted the main course of the story, and all she'd gotten so far were a few sides, if that. She wanted to see the dogs.

It had been over six months since she'd put pen to paper. Now that she finally had a story to write, she was getting impatient. Katie didn't want to be rude, but she really needed some time to watch the dogs, to find their magic. But as she walked up next to Doc about to say something, he raised his fingers against his lips.

Did he just shush me?

Before she could protest, he pointed towards the open field with his other hand. It was the land.

From where Katie stood, they looked down on what appeared to be an empty pasture. A myriad of different trees surrounded it. The land was flat, and quiet. Yet, it almost felt as if all of nature were crowded in around it just waiting for something to happen.

That's when Katie saw him. He was several hundred feet away, so it was too far to be certain, but it looked like the outline of the same man she'd seen earlier.

At first, he was alone as he walked out of a small clearing and into the open field, but seconds later the first dog appeared. He was slightly bigger than the rest, who followed in pairs. By her count there were fifteen dogs, and not once did they break formation, stopping a few paces in front of the man.

After pausing for a few seconds, his back still to the dogs, the man began walking again. He was close enough that Katie could see his left arm at his side, but his right arm was bent up towards the sky, his palm open. Every few seconds he closed his palm into a fist and the dogs stopped. Then he opened his hand again and walked on. He did this for several minutes, until he was about halfway across the field.

Once he reached the middle of the field he closed his hand once more, but kept on walking until he was about ten to twenty feet from the dogs. Then, he turned to face them.

Again, he held his hand out in front of him, this time raising his index finger. He paused for a moment, and pointed to the ground next to him. The lead dog moved almost instantly, jogging over beside him where he then sat down. Katie was almost certain that was also the same dog that had approached her while she'd been playing with the puppies.

The man stood with the single dog by his side, the other fourteen directly in front of him. Several minutes passed before any of them moved. Katie's eyes shot from dog to dog. While they were still too far away to see any details, she could make out that around half of the dogs were slightly smaller than the others. Perhaps younger, she thought. But still none of them moved.

Then the man tapped the dog sitting next to him on the back of the neck, just as she had seen Doc do earlier to Biscuit. The dog followed him over to the others as the man turned his back to them once again. He released his hand, now clenched in a fist in the air, and spoke one single word as he began to walk forward.

"Hike."

The dogs walked in a straight line. Some of the smaller ones seemed hard pressed to keep such a slow pace, as if all they wanted was to break into a run. Occasionally they would break formation, but it was almost as if the man knew when this was happening, despite having his back turned. Whenever a dog would break a few feet away, the man would issue another command and the other dogs would turn right or left, reforming.

Katie sat in silence with Doc, watching the young man repeat this pattern for almost an hour across the entire field. If someone would have traced their steps it would probably look as if they had walked in circles for days.

When it was all over, the man dismissed the dogs one by one the same way they had come, through a slender opening in the tree line. Each of them sprinted away at a feverish pace, the next one following shortly after.

Katie looked down at the pad in her lap. It was as empty as it had been when she'd bought it. It seemed even emptier, somehow. There was something about the dogs, but she couldn't quite put her finger on it. She had never seen animals move with such unity, but she was at a loss for words. Which, for her, hadn't been unusual lately.

Doc straightened from where he'd leaned against the tree and Katie heard a quiet groan. She didn't know if it was Doc stretching or the tree responding in relief from the shift in weight.

Still not ready to leave and desperately wanting to get at least some words on the page, Katie turned to him. "Do you mind if I just sit here a while and write?"

Since it was mostly a rhetorical question, she didn't expect Doc to object. But he did.

"Actually, Miss Price, I don't think that would be such a good idea."

Katie's heart sank. *Is he kicking me out? Did I do something wrong?*

She was about to start apologizing for whatever it was she might have done. She hadn't driven for nearly a week straight just to turn around and head back home.

"Unfortunately, it's almost dark, and I just don't think it'd be a good idea for you to be out here all alone, with the coyotes and all," Doc explained.

Katie was momentarily relieved she hadn't worn out her welcome, but then she realized she had another problem. It was nearly dark, and she was in a small town with nowhere to stay.

6

BY THE TIME DOC AND KATIE made it back to the house, the sun was already fading below the tree line.

Katie looked down at her watch. It was nearly six o'clock. She tugged lightly on the hour-hand pin on the side of the watch and spun it around until it was exactly one hour later. She had forgotten to add an hour after she crossed the last time-zone change in Georgia. So, it was nearly seven o'clock and she had no place to stay, nor any real plans for what she might do next.

"Everything all right, Miss Price?" Doc interjected.

"Oh. Yes. I just need to get going, I think. I didn't really plan this trip out as much as I probably should have. Would it be all right if I came back again tomorrow morning? Maybe just to watch the dogs?"

"Well, unfortunately I've got some bad news."

"The dogs wouldn't even know I'm here," she began to explain.

Doc chuckled. "Don't be silly. You are more than welcome to watch and write about the dogs as much as you'd like. However, there is a problem that is a bit more practical. Mrs. Davis runs the only motel in town, which is more or less a bed and breakfast large enough for just a few people. Normally I'd tell you to take a left on your way out of here, a right on Calhoun after about half a mile, and you'd run right into her place after another couple miles. But you'd be out of luck if you did that because Mrs. Davis is currently on her way to her brother's funeral in Sumter. Sad thing, really."

Doc turned towards his house as if he was finished speaking. As he took the first step, without even turning around, he simply said, "Supper is in thirty minutes."

Katie started to protest. "Thank you, but..."

"You can drive about an hour to Camden or Florence and possibly find something there, or a couple hours to Columbia if you'd prefer. But you best get goin' before it gets too dark. You don't want to get lost in the middle of nowhere."

The screen door clattered behind him as he stepped inside, and left Katie standing outside a stranger's house in a small town in South Carolina.

Katie just stood there, looking down at the scuffs and stains on her favorite Burberry boots. The bottom of her jeans were spotted with dirt, but she was glad she had changed. Her eyes traced the worn lines below them along the porch floor, down the stairs, and onto the dirt road. She looked out towards the winding path that she knew led back to a paved road.

A pot or pan clanged against something metal and she turned back to the screen door. Her hand reached out towards the rusted iron handle and rested there for a minute. Then she pulled the door open.

When Katie entered the house, she could instantly hear the sizzle of something on the stove. The kitchen was only a few steps into the house, and directly to her left.

"Breakfast for dinner," Doc said with a grin as he used a pair of tongs to flip a couple strips of bacon over. "You can set your stuff down on the tansu."

Katie guessed he was referring to the chest of drawers behind the dining room table. Her guess was confirmed as Doc nodded when she set her bag on it.

Just above the tansu was a large painting of a bonsai tree, hand stitched into what appeared to be some type of wool fabric. Below the tree was the image of a boy who had tripped over a large rock. He lay on his back looking up at the tree. Katie stood as motionless as the boy and stared at the mural.

Without looking up from the three frying pans on the stove Doc said, "Nana korobi, ya oki."

Katie glanced over at him. "What does that mean?"

"I never figured it out," Doc said, laughing aloud. "But when I was stationed in Japan, I used to sit and stare at that thing for days on end. I don't really know why. I guess partially because I didn't have much else to do, and partially because it was hung outside one of the only restaurants I could afford to eat at off base.

"One night after I had finished my dinner, a Japanese man—I still don't know his name to this day—walked up and handed me that thing, all rolled up with two ribbons tied around each end. Before I could say thank you he said, *'Nana korobi, ya oki,'* and walked away."

Doc flipped the pancakes over one last time. "That should do it."

He put one pancake, a large spoonful of scrambled eggs, and two pieces of bacon on each plate. As he walked them over to the table, Katie noticed a third plate that still sat empty on the counter.

"Shall we eat?" he said.

She hadn't realized how hungry she was until Doc set the plate down in front of her. The food smelled amazing, and she couldn't remember the last time she'd had a home-cooked meal. The eggs were like soft little yellow pillows, and the pancakes still hot enough to melt a small slice of butter that she spread on top of them. But the best part looked to be the strips of bacon. They looked so greasy they might slip out of her hands when she picked them up, but they were delicious. It was a nice change from her California diet of salad or sushi.

Doc walked back into the kitchen and grabbed a glass bottle of Aunt Jemima syrup. "Can't exactly eat pancakes without this, now can we?"

Katie forced a smile, suddenly less at ease. As Doc sat down across from her, she realized a somewhat alarming truth: she was eating dinner with a complete stranger.

Less than a week ago, she'd been alone on her porch on the coast of California getting in arguments with her agent about her impending story deadline. And now, well...now she was as far away from home as she had been in years, eating breakfast for dinner with a stranger.

Doc must have noticed something was wrong, because he stopped eating for a brief moment after shoving what seemed like half a pancake in his mouth in one bite. Or perhaps not. After a swig of some milk, he shoved the other half in.

They ate the rest of the meal in silence. Katie figured that food was the one thing that actually prevented Doc from being his usually talkative self. For a moment, the silence seemed to amplify the fact that she had found herself in a somewhat uncomfortable situation, but the more she ate the more she calmed down, until finally she was thankful for the silence.

Her mind had been so loud the entire day. Screaming, *Find the story! Notice the details! Find the story!* Dinner calmed her a bit. Perhaps because she knew there was a story here in this little town, on this little farm...or perhaps because for the first time in months there was not just silence around her, but silence forming within her. That was, until Doc finished his meal a few minutes later.

"There's a few things I've got to finish before I turn in. If you don't mind, Kyle will show you to the cottage."

"Kyle?" Katie questioned. "The cottage?"

"Ah, yes. Well, the cottage is technically the only house on this property. As I'm sure by now you've noticed, we're sitting in a double-wide trailer. The cottage however, is far from a trailer. Or at least I like to think so. It's not exactly finished, but I think it will do the trick. I meant to show you earlier, but my understanding was you wanted to spend the afternoon watching the dogs, so I had to cut our grand tour a little short."

Doc paused for a moment. He was only several feet from Katie, but to her his mind felt distant again. She heard the screen door clatter shut for the second time that night, which was enough to break Doc out of his momentary trance.

As Katie turned around, he said, "Miss Price, my nephew Kyle. Kyle, our guest, Miss Price."

This was the third time Katie had seen Kyle in the past few hours, but the first time she ever really *saw* him.

He was young; he couldn't be more than a year or two older than her. He was slightly taller than average, maybe an inch shy of six foot. His hair was dark, but covered mostly by a baseball hat, the kind that Katie saw truckers wearing during her stops along the way to South Carolina. On the front, the words "One Pace" were inscribed. The stitching on the letters was starting to come undone, and it was evident they had been hand sewn, as she noticed several knots indicating a start-stop point.

As Kyle stepped inside, he glanced at her for a moment and she noticed a few subtle brown freckles on his face, mixed in with a bit of dirt. His shoulders were broad and the top button of his rust-orange Henley shirt was unbuttoned. The sleeves were pushed up a few inches and she could see the muscles in his arms tighten as he wiped his hands on a white rag. But there was nothing more telling than his eyes. They were not a sharp blue, or a sea green, but rather a deep brown. And they were calm.

Katie went to extend her hand, but before she was able to do so, Kyle pinched the brim of his ball cap and greeted her.

"Miss," he said. He pulled down on his hat and nodded in her direction, his other hand stuffing the rag into his back pocket.

Katie smiled casually back at him. He seemed somewhat shy, she thought. It was unexpected after watching him command the dogs with such confidence earlier.

"Miss Price will be staying with us for..." Doc said, turning to Katie to answer his question.

Katie thought about his offer for a moment. It wasn't exactly every day that she drove across the country to some random town and bunked with locals. This wasn't the seventies. Today people locked their doors, didn't let their kids play outside alone, and above all didn't trust anyone.

She looked through the screen door towards her car, now covered in dust from the dirt roads. Then she thought about what her agent had said just a few days ago. *You have three weeks to get me a draft.* She didn't have much choice.

"Just a few days, if that's all right," Katie supplied.

"Miss Price will be staying with us for just a few days, then," Doc finished. "I've got some things to finish up before it gets too dark. Dinner is on the stove after you show Miss Price to the cottage."

Kyle's expression changed to what Katie perceived as slightly irritated after Doc uttered those last words. But before he could protest or comment Doc added, "I just happened to check on the cottage a couple days ago so I know the water still runs, but you will need to grab some towels and sheets. Don't forget to open the bedroom window for her. You know that latch sticks."

Doc turned to Katie. "Breakfast is just before dawn at this table."

With that he smiled, winked, and walked out the backdoor, leaving Katie in an uncomfortable silence with yet another stranger.

She suspected she might be getting a barrage of questions from Kyle, wondering why there was some strange girl standing in his house. So, she started to think up answers.

I told Dr. Anderson I would drive to the nearest hotel, but he insisted I stay here.

I'm a writer from California.

Don't worry, I won't get in your way. I just want to watch the dogs. I think there's a great story to tell about them.

But as she stood there waiting for all those questions, Kyle just turned around and walked back out the same door he'd come in, leaving Katie alone in the kitchen.

Katie scooped up her purse and hurried out after him.

"Dr. Anderson said you were going to show me where the cottage was?" she asked, trailing behind him.

Kyle continued walking.

"Excuse me...Kyle?" Katie said.

No response. He just kept walking until he had crossed the dirt path in front of the house and disappeared into the barn.

"Okay...I suppose I should have expected this much," she said to herself as she stood alone. The night breeze was cool, and it cut right through her sweater, giving her chills.

She started to make her way towards her car when she heard a voice behind her.

"That way leads off the property. This way leads to the cottage."

She turned around and saw Kyle walking out of the barn and away from her in the opposite direction. Behind him trotted the same black dog she'd seen earlier that day.

For a moment, Katie contemplated getting in the car and just driving off. Dr. Anderson had been nice and helpful, but it seemed very clear that Kyle didn't want her here for whatever reason. She was already standing near her car, and the fact that it was nearly dark made her even more nervous about the whole situation.

Does he know I'm here to write about the dogs? Does he not want me near them? Does he just not like people in general?

The more she thought about it, the more she heard the voice of her agent again.

One month, Katie. That's all the time I can buy you.

She reached into the backseat of her car and pulled out her suitcase. There was a problem immediately —plastic suitcase tires don't roll on dirt roads. She sighed to herself, then threw her purse over her shoulder, pushed the suitcase handle back down, picked it up by the side strap, and took off after Kyle and his dog. The suitcase banged against her leg with nearly every step.

The cottage wasn't exactly right around the corner, like Doc had implied. At least, it didn't feel that way to Katie after half carrying and half dragging her suitcase behind Kyle, who hardly appeared to notice.

Just the opposite was the black dog who trailed them by about fifty paces. Katie could hear his heavy panting with each step, and any time she turned to look at him, she found his jet-black eyes locked on her.

Figures that the dog wants more to do with me than the man.

Kyle pulled a key from his pocket and fit it into the brass door handle. She couldn't help but wonder why they even bothered locking the door. Looking around at nothing but empty land, she couldn't imagine there was another person living within a mile.

Katie followed Kyle into the house as the door creaked open, her suitcase finally finding flat wood floors to roll across.

She wasn't sure what to expect as she took several steps into the house, but after eating dinner in Doc's double-wide she didn't expect much. Yet again, she found herself surprised.

She'd anticipated dusty countertops or unfinished rooms, possibly even cobwebs or some musty odor hanging around the house. What she saw was none of the above.

It was easy to see that no one was living here, but she couldn't understand why not. The first thing she noticed was the flooring. It was dark with lots of knots and twisted grain, but it was beautiful. The crease between each board was deep, almost as if every single piece had been cut to fit in that exact spot.

The living room was immediately to her right—the direction Kyle had gone. She started to follow, but the dining room table to her left caught her eye.

The table looked antique. It was round, solid, with no split down the middle to add a rectangular leaf for more guests. There were three chairs arranged around it on one side, but on the other side sat a hand-carved wooden bench that was connected to the wall and sat just below a single-pane window.

Kyle opened the large wooden trunk at the foot of the bed, as Katie walked in behind him.

The bed was empty, but it was huge. A large four-post frame nearly consumed the room, and Katie almost tripped as she tried to squeeze between Kyle and the dresser.

He pulled two sheets and several pillow cases out of the trunk and tossed them on the bed. He latched the trunk closed and walked out of the room. She assumed he was leaving her like before, without even a goodbye.

After testing the water in the bathroom she walked back into the bedroom to find Kyle neatly tucking the bed sheet around each corner of the bed. His movements were meticulous. He fanned open the top sheet and let it float down again, running his hands to each corner until there were no creases. She thought of her house back home—unpacked boxes scattered throughout the house, furniture randomly placed from room to room, and the only beds made were the ones no one slept in. Watching him work made her feel like a slob.

He walked over to the window as he finished putting the last pillowcase on.

"You don't need to worry about the window," she said rubbing her cold hands together.

Kyle looked over to her, his eyes resting on hers for a moment. "Miss," he said, again tipping his hat like earlier.

"You can call me Katie," she blurted as he turned to leave.

He stopped for a moment, his back already to her. "Yes ma'am," he replied, and walked out the door.

7

WHEN KATIE WOKE UP the next morning she almost forgot she wasn't in her own bed back in San Diego. She stretched out against the cool white sheets and looked down at her watch.

9:54 a.m. That can't be right.

She checked her cell phone, but it was dead.

She ran to the window, threw open the drapes, and lifted the window open—or tried to. It didn't budge. She tried again. And again. Nothing. Not even a creak.

Still in her pajamas—light blue pants and a long-sleeved button-up top with little images of baby bears—she headed for the front door.

When she got to the front door she looked down at her bare feet, ran back to her room, and slipped her boots on. The legs of her pajamas bunched up against them.

When she got to the front door again she swung it open and took the front steps one by one, walking about twenty feet from the house until she could clearly see the sun to the east. It was just already climbing the sky over the tree line. Her watch was right.

"I guess you're not much of a breakfast person," Katie heard from behind her.

A bit startled and not expecting anyone, she nearly screamed. She relaxed slightly when she turned and saw Doc leaning under the shade of a large oak tree, Biscuit sitting calmly by his side. He had a knife in his right hand and was carving the top of a long stick that he held braced against his left leg.

"I'm sorry. I meant to be up, but my phone died. And that was my only alarm."

Doc laughed heartily to himself. "Well, can't do much about breakfast, but if you're lookin' to see those dogs today you better get a move on. He only works them half a day on Sundays."

Doc pointed to a trail between two large trees about fifty yards away. "Follow that trail through the trees. Take a hard left when you see the opening and keep walking until you see 'em. They'll be out there about another two hours or so." Then he walked back down the dirt path towards his house, turning to Biscuit every few yards to say something that Katie couldn't quite make out.

Katie was partly disappointed that she'd missed breakfast. She was relieved, however, that she at least had a couple hours to watch the dogs.

She hurried back inside to get ready. She plugged her cell phone in, grabbed her makeup bag and headed straight for the bathroom. She pulled back the curtain and lifted her leg over the high sidewall of the claw-foot tub and stepped in. Two minutes later, she understood why people recommended a cold shower in the morning to wake up. It was terrible and refreshing all at the same time.

With a towel wrapped around her, she lay her suitcase on the floor in front of the closet and unzipped it, then lay her clothes out all over the bed. For a moment she considered hanging them up, until she realized there were no hangers. Instead, she re-zipped her suitcase and stood a few feet away from the bed to analyze her choices. Looking at the clothes in front of her, Katie wished she hadn't packed in such a hurry. Without many options to choose from, she settled on the same pair of jeans from yesterday and a maroon knit sweater. She dried her hair quickly, grabbed her only pair of boots, tucked her notebook under her arm, and headed in the direction Doc had pointed her towards.

The copse of trees surrounding the cottage must have insulated the cool air a bit, because just a few steps out of the trail, a chilly wind collided with Katie. It felt like a cold shower all over again, but the more she walked the more she welcomed the breeze. She turned to her left just as Doc had instructed and looked out to an endless horizon of green land.

The terrain appeared flat from a distance, but as she walked she could easily feel the unevenness of the earth. At least this morning she wasn't lugging around her suitcase.

After several minutes of walking, she found her eyes wandering more and more over the endless landscape in front of her. It was almost hypnotic. For a moment she didn't even realize that she was no longer on flat ground, but walking slightly downhill, and when she looked behind her she noticed she hadn't been on flat ground for some time.

And then she saw them.

When she had first seen the dogs there had only been fifteen, many of whom seemed to be very young. But now in front of her were over twenty dogs, excluding the five puppies from Biscuit's litter.

Unlike yesterday, though, there was no organization, no neat rows of dogs marching or following orders—just twenty or so dogs, and one man. Playing.

Katie sat down in the distance, thinking she might be able to watch unnoticed.

She opened her notepad and scribbled the date in the upper right-hand corner of the first page.

She watched each dog intently and started to write down descriptions. Not only how they looked, but how they moved, how they interacted, how they responded to one another and to Kyle. There were so many dogs that it was a challenge getting the details down, especially when trying to differentiate between several who looked almost identical.

Determined to get it right, she watched more closely as the dogs circled Kyle. At first their movement seemed random, as if the dogs were just playing with one another and Kyle as they saw fit. But by the time she had made it halfway through describing each dog, she'd begun to notice a pattern. She was close enough to hear the dogs bark and yip occasionally, but not nearly close enough to make out any words Kyle said—if he was saying anything at all.

As she watched the exchange between Kyle and the dogs, she realized he must be calling them over one by one. She couldn't figure out how, as it didn't appear that he was speaking to them, but after several minutes a different dog would approach.

Kyle stood up, interlocked his hands, and stretched them towards the sky. He leaned to the left, then to the right. Some of the dogs were lying down panting, some of them rolling around, some even pressing their faces into the grass and dirt.

Directly behind Kyle, two dogs played. Katie let out a quiet laugh as one kept spinning its backside into the other.

When Kyle knelt back down he faced the two that Katie had been watching and they both stopped. Ears perked, tails wagging, bodies wriggling, they approached Kyle. But as the dogs neared, she noticed a drastic change in behavior. Their ears tucked tightly against their necks, their heads dropped, and they stepped as if they were walking over broken glass. They didn't seem upset, but attentive. Serious.

When they were within arms' reach, both dogs sat. Kyle leaned down and instead of placing his hand on either dog's head or back, he placed one hand between each of the dog's front legs, against the chest. Again, the dogs' demeanor changed. Their tight shoulders relaxed, their ears stood tall, and their faces rose to meet his. They almost looked regal. This was the only time Katie thought Kyle might be speaking to the dogs, but his back was always to her and she was just too far away to know for sure. It was a beautiful moment to watch, even though she truly had no clue what was happening.

It wasn't until she heard panting that the moment ended. For a minute, she thought that she had subconsciously moved closer to Kyle and the dogs, but she hadn't. And then, for the second time that day, she nearly screamed. Seated next to her, panting, was the same large black dog from yesterday.

He paid almost no attention to her. His eyes were deep and black and distant as he watched the other dogs.

Katie just stared at the dog for a moment, until finally he turned his attention from the group and looked directly at her. His mouth closed and the panting stopped. His right ear straightened in her direction, but his left ear turned independently towards the other dogs still playing.

At least this is an improvement over growling at me…I hope.

The wind shifted slightly and his nostrils flared, likely picking up more of her scent.

As she sat staring at the dog, she couldn't help but want to speak. She felt as though he looked at her not only with curiosity, but with some greater knowing, almost as if to say, "I have the answers you seek, but you have not yet earned them." She felt as though the dog knew everything about her, while she knew nothing about him.

She held his gaze until the wind picked up again. This time, he turned his head back towards Kyle and the other dogs, and without warning trotted off—though not in the direction of the dogs, but following the same subtle ridgeline on which Katie was sitting.

"Where are you going?" she whispered.

She turned back to see Kyle walk several feet away from the dogs. He snapped his fingers one time. The sound was soft from where she was sitting, but it was distinct. Most of the dogs stopped playing, or sniffing the ground. Those lying down stood. Then he held his hand in front of his body and the dogs sat. All but three, that is. Those dogs stopped what they were doing but stood confused, or perhaps defiant.

Katie expected Kyle to snap his fingers again, but instead he walked over to the three dogs standing and corrected them individually until they were sitting like the others. He walked back to the front of the dogs, made another motion with his hands, and walked back the same way he had come. The dogs followed, some of them walking behind him, some to the side, and even a couple in front. The white of the underside of their tails danced in the sunlight as they left.

She jotted down a few more notes and then folded the notebook closed, sliding the pencil down the wired binding before she followed behind them.

The walk back was peaceful as Katie followed Kyle and the dogs. They travelled a small path formed by tall pines on the right side – pinus palustris, if Katie remembered correctly – and scattered oaks on the left. The path opened up into a field three times as large as the one they'd been in. Some of the dogs looked back at her occasionally, but for the most part they didn't veer from the pack. By the time she reached the barn, Kyle had already put each dog back in its respective pen. Katie started to walk towards him. She had so many questions still, but Doc interrupted her.

"And how is your day going so far, Miss Price?" Doc asked. He was sitting in the same rocking chair she had found him in yesterday.

"It's going well," she said, tapping her hand against her notebook. "Though I'm sorry for missing breakfast this morning." She had forgotten just how hungry she was until she mentioned food. It had to be well past lunch and she hadn't eaten a single thing, which she noticed was starting to turn into an unpleasant theme lately. It may have not been that unusual for her to miss a meal or two in San Diego, but she wasn't walking around thousands of acres of land then.

Katie walked up the steps and sat in the empty rocking chair next to Doc.

She just sat there for a moment breathing in the country air. The fresh scent of pine resin on a morning breeze, the mildly sweet smell of meadow hay spread around the barn, and the leafy scent of a thousand sunflowers. Then she asked, "May I ask you a question?"

"I believe you just did," Doc said, taking a sip of his lemonade.

Katie smiled. "Well, may I ask you two more?"

"That would mean you've got one left."

"This morning when I was watching Kyle with the dogs, I noticed something he was doing. It was hard to make out from a distance, and I didn't want to get too close because I wasn't sure if he was training them seriously today or just playing with them. But, anyways, I saw him do this one thing. He would call the dog over to him, or so it seemed, and then he would place his hand on the dog's chest and just kneel there in front of the dog."

"Hand over heart."

Katie looked at Doc, scrunching her nose up slightly.

"Your question, I assume, is what exactly was Kyle doing with the dogs? And the answer is something called hand over heart."

"What exactly is hand over heart?"

"Well, that would be your fourth question, and one better suited for Kyle."

8

KATIE LOOKED UP from her conversation with Doc as Kyle walked out of the barn and towards the house. He was busy rolling his right sleeve back up to match his left as his boots crunched over the dirt path.

When he reached the top of the steps he lifted his ball cap up by the brim and set it back farther on his head, as though his hat had been working hard and needed a break.

He locked eyes on Katie and slowly looked her over. It was eerily similar to the way the black dog had looked at her yesterday. Almost as if he wanted to know if she would be a threat. Not to him so much, but to the dogs.

He's protective, she thought.

He looked back to Doc. "I have a little work to do around the barn."

Doc set his lemonade down next to him. The glass was empty and the large square ice cubes rattled against it when it hit the table. He reached for the large walking stick that was leaning against the faded yellow siding, and ran his hand along the indentations in the wood.

"Wait one second," Doc said as he walked in side. A few seconds later he walked back out with a gray rectangular object in his hand. Doc ran his hands over the coarse features. "You got another whetstone anywhere? This thing couldn't sharpen a star in the night."

Katie smiled at the expression, making a mental note to jot that down later.

Kyle pulled the brim of his hat back down with his right hand, straightened the back with his left, and turned to walk back to the barn.

Doc stood, walking stick in hand. "Miss Price would like to spend a little more time with the dogs today. Perhaps she could help you out."

"If it's all right with you," Katie added quickly. "I don't even need to do anything, just watch really."

Kyle looked back at her, his eyes digging into hers. "How do you expect to write about something you don't understand? And how do you expect to understand something by simply watching?"

She was so taken aback at his words that she didn't know what to say or do.

She absolutely hated the way he looked at her. It was like his eyes judged her as a person even as his words judged her as a writer. But the truth was, he was partly right: how could she possibly write anything worth reading just by watching? She needed to be with the dogs, to be around them and interact with them. To understand their personalities, their strengths, their shortcomings. To find out the answer to the one question that kept repeating over and over in her mind. *What is so special about these dogs, anyway?*

From somewhere behind them a phone rang, breaking the silence, and Doc walked quickly into the house—almost urgently, Katie thought. She could clearly make out his voice as it carried through the house and onto the front porch.

"Hello. Calm. Mr. Perry, calm. I will be there in fifteen minutes. Do nothing until I get there. Nothing."

Doc walked back out with a coat in one hand and a dark green battle bag in the other. There was a white circle with a red cross in the center on one side of the bag. It looked like a type of army medical bag. Doc looked at Kyle as he descended the steps. "Mrs. Perry is in labor. I'll be back when I'm back. You'll be cooking dinner for Miss Price tonight."

Katie went to tell him that wasn't necessary, but a quick glance from him stopped her.

"Keep Miss Price with you while you finish your work. I'm sure she has lots of questions about the dogs." His tone was commanding and stopped the protest Katie was almost certain Kyle was on the verge of uttering.

Doc turned back to Katie. "There's a sandwich and some lemonade in the fridge. Feel free to help yourself."

With that, Doc hopped in his old blue and white short-wide GMC and drove off.

CHAPTER 9

THE BARN ENTRANCE consisted of heavy double doors on a rusted, sliding track. The wheels had dug a rut into the ground, which had the effect of causing the door to tilt and bow slightly. Each door was pulled wide open and secured to the wall with a latch.

Kyle was a few paces ahead of Katie when she reached the threshold. He peered into the barn and looked around momentarily, then spun quickly to face her.

He stared straight at her, so close and still that she could even make out the small hazel prisms in his brown eyes. He leaned in closer.

Katie jumped back. "Umm, what are you doing?"

"You smell," he said plainly.

"I what?" Katie asked, her face flushed with embarrassment and anger.

"Your perfume."

"Oh. Sorry, it's a habit."

Kyle began to unfold a red bandana that wrapped around his wrist. He wiped the sweat from his face and neck with it and then folded it in half, so that it resembled a triangle.

"Turn around."

Katie was a little reluctant, but obliged. "You're not going to do anything weird are you?"

"Not any weirder than randomly driving across the country to write about dogs you hadn't even heard about till you met the local grocery clerk," he said.

She thought she could hear a smile in his words.

Before Katie could respond, Kyle wrapped his arms around her, draping the bandana in front of her like a necklace and tying it gently behind her neck. The small hairs on his arm brushed against her skin, giving her goose bumps.

"The dogs will know you first by scent. Even with this on you'll smell...different. But it's better that they recognize something familiar about you."

"That one black dog didn't seem to mind the smell today."

Kyle gently pressed his hands into her shoulders, spinning her back around. Katie fought to stay focused on something other than his firm touch as his fingers remained wrapped around her shoulders.

"He's...different," Kyle said.

Katie's eyes followed his hands as they returned to his waist. She forced herself to look back at his face. "Well then, what about the buyers who come to look at the dogs? Doc mentioned something about them."

"They never enter the barn. The dogs are only shown training in the field."

Kyle looked into the barn and then back to Katie. "Do not speak to the dogs. Do not touch the dogs, even if they approach."

"Are they dangerous?"

She thought she saw a playful spark in his eyes. "That will depend on you," he said, reminding her of a comment Doc had made the day before.

Katie expected the barn to smell like wet dog, but it surprisingly had almost no aroma, save from a bit of freshly scattered hay on the ground. It was also a lot larger than it appeared from the outside. The horse stalls had been turned into makeshift dog pens, and it was probably over a hundred feet from one end of the structure to the other.

The door on the other side of the barn was wide open like the one she and Kyle had just walked through, and there was a narrow skylight that stretched the full span of the roof. This was enough to light the barn for the most part, but towards the back of each pen it was still dark.

Kyle motioned at Katie to follow him. They walked down one side of the barn and then down the other, ending up where they had originally entered.

Most of the dogs sat completely still in their pens, ears perked and their eyes focused on her—except for several of the younger ones, who couldn't have been more than six months old. They paced in their pens. Some even stood up on their hind legs, wrapping their front paws over the top board as Kyle and Katie passed. Kyle corrected each one with a single word: "Off."

Katie tried to take in as much information as possible, but her mind was racing. It had been a long time since she had been this excited about a story.

First, she tried to get a rough count. She'd come up with twenty-three earlier in the field, but this time she only saw twenty-two, plus the five puppies.

She looked from dog to dog as quickly as she could. Each of their coats were made up of three different colors—predominately white with large black spots and ginger markings; black with white markings on the feet, forehead, or chest; and solid black.

She started to look at their fur, as some of them had short cropped coats, while others had longer fur. All the coats looked thick like that of a husky, but the texture looked different. It was like being in an art museum and not being able to touch the paintings. Katie wanted to reach out and touch one of the dogs, to feel their coarse coats. She was interrupted when Kyle came to her with a shovel and a bucket.

He held them out towards her and she took them, one in each hand, holding them away from her body as if they might try to bite her.

"The pups need their final deworming. I'll take them to the house where we keep all the meds. They're not old enough yet to make it through the night without making a mess. Scoop it up and toss it in the bucket. Make sure you check along the back of the pen. They don't like to make a mess where they sleep, but occasionally it happens."

Katie looked down at the bucket and realized the brown spots scattered along the sides weren't dirt.

"You're kidding, right?"

"When you're done you can rake the hay out, as well."

Kyle walked across the barn and returned with a wheelbarrow and a rake. "Put it in here and I'll bring a new bale in to spread."

"You're serious?"

Kyle didn't say a word.

"I was kind of hoping to spend some time with the dogs. So that I could actually write about them."

Kyle stood still for a moment in front of Katie, just looking at her. He rubbed his arm across his forehead, catching a few beads of sweat. He repeated what he had said earlier, but this time Katie didn't feel like the words were meant to hurt her, but to help her understand. "How can you write about something you don't understand?"

"Well, I was kind of hoping I could learn from you. Maybe watch you with the dogs."

"You watched me with the dogs for hours earlier today. What do you think more watching is going to do?"

Katie hadn't been sure that Kyle had seen her earlier, but now she found herself a little embarrassed. As if watching him play with the dogs was a secret ritual that she was never meant to see.

"Well, I figured I could watch them up close and really get to know them."

Kyle's hands went to his hips as he shook his head with disapproval. "Come with me," he said.

She followed him across the barn until they were standing in front of an empty pen. He unpinned the latch, opened it, and walked in.

"Tell me what you see."

Katie hesitated. The pen didn't look much different than any of the others. She looked around, knowing this must be some type of test.

There must be something about this pen.

"I don't know. There's no dog in this pen. It's empty."

Kyle walked out of the pen, latching it closed behind him, and stood directly in front of another.

"And what do you see here?"

Katie quickly walked over and stood next to him. There was a simple wooden name post nailed to the top board. It read, "Belle."

In the back corner of the pen was a single dog. She had a shaggy white coat with large black spots. Her head was black as well, and accented with symmetrical tan markings on her eyebrows and jaw. Even lying down, Katie could see the bulge in her stomach.

"She's pregnant."

"Yes. She is. But what do you know about her?"

Katie thought to herself, *Well, I know she's pregnant...*

"You know nothing about her. Understanding comes only through experience."

With that, Kyle walked back to the pen containing the five puppies and marched them out of the barn.

Katie just stood there silently. She looked at Belle until the dog finally lost interest and laid her head back on a patch of hay on the floor.

How is cleaning up dog poop going to help me understand these dogs? Nothing he said made any sense.

But what other options did she have? She looked down at the date on her watch. In less than three weeks she owed her agent a rough draft. She wanted to sit on a bench and write about each dog as Kyle trained them, not clean up after them. She picked up the shovel leaning against the top rail and the dirty bucket that lay next to it. At this point, she didn't really have a choice.

10

AFTER FALLING ASLEEP immediately after dinner, the next morning Katie awoke with ease. Shoveling dog poop and raking hay may not be hard work for a lot of people, but it was the only work Katie had done besides write in years. Her arms and shoulders were sore and her feet still hurt from walking around the property. She raised her arms above her head to stretch and turned from side to side. Even that little motion caused pain in her sides.

She would have preferred to wake up to a nice hot bath, but she prepared herself for the shock of the cold water as she stepped into the shower. Unbelievably, the first drop of water against her skin was warm. Not hot, but definitely not cold, either.

As the warm water ran through her hair and down the small of her back, she almost forgot that she had gotten up early to see the dogs. She was hoping that Kyle would repay her hard work yesterday with a little bit of time to watch him train the dogs today, and maybe even answer some questions. A few minutes later, that hope was gone.

After she got dressed she made her way to the kitchen table, where she had begun to lay out her notes thus far for the story. Something caught her eye. As she walked past the front door she noticed a yellow piece of legal paper stuffed between the door and the doorjamb.

She opened the door and pulled the note inside. It was folded meticulously in three even halves and on one side, in all capital letters, was her full name: *Katherine Price*.

She unfolded the note, held it in front of her, and read:

November 5, 2007

I fixed the hot water.

Breakfast is wrapped in tinfoil and sitting in the oven.

I will be gone most of the day with the dogs.

Medicine chests are sitting on the steps. Please clean them out and inventory.

Rigging is hanging at the far end of the barn on hooks. Please clean and inventory.

Lunch is at noon. Dinner is at 6 p.m.

Doc will be gone again.

Katie groaned as she crumpled the paper in her hand and tossed it on the table with her other notes.

For the next two days, she woke up to find a new note on the door each morning. *Clean the nameplates, check the pens for any loose boards, prepare the food, clean out the water bowls, organize the files.* No matter how early she woke, a fresh piece of paper was there with a list of things to do for that day. None of which ever included spending any time with the dogs.

She had tried pleading with Doc, but since he was the only doctor in town, he was gone most of the time dealing with more important problems, especially since Mrs. Perry's baby had been born. That left Katie to spend most of the days doing chores by herself. Well, not entirely by herself.

Belle was fifty-seven days into her gestation period, which Katie had learned from the scattered conversations she'd had with Kyle over the past few days. That meant she was due any day now. That also meant that Kyle had to leave Belle behind each morning when he left with the dogs.

Kyle had quarantined the dog, though, so it wasn't like she was by Katie's side. No one was to enter her pen, except Kyle. Period.

Still, it was nice to feel Belle's presence whenever Katie had a chore in or around the barn. Every now and then she would stop outside Belle's pen and just talk to the dog. Sometimes, she talked to her about the story and the progress she was making, or about potential plot lines. Other times, she asked Belle about Bishopville, or Doc, or the other dogs. Or occasionally Kyle. *All right, more than occasionally,* Katie thought grudgingly.

At the end of the third day, Katie hung the empty silver pail on a nail near the barn entrance. She took her time as she walked towards Belle's pen. She stopped at the first pen and traced her hand over the wooden name plates that hung from the gate. Saint, Solomon, Samson, Rev, and Angel. All the names of Biscuit's puppies. They were likely sleeping under Doc's house at the moment, or perhaps chasing Biscuit around. It seemed odd that Kyle let the puppies roam around during the day, but he was the expert, not her.

Cotton, Peanut, and Apple were the next three. Katie referred to them as the "crop dogs," because she assumed they were all named after crops in South Carolina.

There was an empty pen next to Cotton and then there was Belle, towards the middle of the barn.

Kyle and the dogs would likely be back soon and they'd find their food and water bowls filled and waiting.

Katie sat down and pulled out her notebook, which she had jammed between one of the slats in front of Belle's pen. Katie leaned her back against the smooth wood and pulled her knees to her chest to use as a writing desk. She heard Belle get up, pad over to the gate, and lie down just behind Katie. Only a one-inch piece of timber separated them. It had become a sort of ritual for Katie and Belle over the past couple days.

"Hey, girl," Katie said, turning towards Belle. She slid her hand through the space just above the toe board and rested it on Belle's side. Her hand rose and fell with each of Belle's breaths.

"You have any wonderful dreams while I was out there sweeping floors, scrubbing feed bowls, and re-bedding stalls?" Belle looked up and let out an audible breath through her nose. Katie moved her fingers back and forth behind the dog's soft ears.

"I know what you mean. Every day can't be full of dreams."

Katie turned back around and jotted down a few notes. The sun was low and she could see the individual rays of light pour into the barn. Little specks of hay and dust floated amongst the light. It would make a beautiful cover, if she ever actually finished the book.

"I just don't get it," Katie started again, turning the conversation to the topic she'd been dwelling on most lately. "What does he have against me being here? He feeds me all these lines about, 'you can't have understanding without experience.' But how am I supposed to get any experience when he takes all the dogs with him and leaves me here alone?"

Katie looked down at Belle. "You know what I mean."

She looked around the barn for a few minutes in silence, thinking about the whole thing. "What would you do if you were me?" Belle groaned as she shifted her weight atop the hay. "I'm sorry, girl. You have bigger problems, huh? I'm sure I'll figure something out."

Katie leaned her head back against one of the horizontal boards and closed her eyes. She was exhausted. Having forgotten her train of thought, she set her notepad and pencil down, and let her mind wander. It didn't take more than a few minutes for her to fall asleep on the barn floor.

11

"MISS PRICE," KYLE SAID. "Miss Price."

Katie opened her eyes to find Kyle squatting a few feet away from her.

"Miss Price," he said again.

She leaned to the side to grab her notebook and quickly wiped what felt like a few drops of drool from her lip.

Oh God, please tell me he did not see that.

"I'm sorry. I must have fallen asleep."

"Dinner is ready," he said. He stood and reached out his hand.

She leaned forward and took it, then paused at the feel of his warm fingers. She could feel his calluses on the sides of her hands and the strength in his grip as he pulled her to her feet. Her weight shifted forward slightly as she stood, and she was suddenly very close to him.

Why is he even being nice to me? Is this him being nice to me? I don't know why I even care.

Dinner was already on the table when they walked into the house. Katie looked around for Doc, but saw no sign of him.

"Doc out again tonight?"

"One of Mr. Willis' cows had a problem birthing," Kyle said.

"Is there anything he doesn't do?"

Kyle looked back at her from the kitchen, and thought for a minute. "Not really." He poured two glasses of lemonade and sat down across from her at the table.

Kyle cut his chicken into small rectangular pieces and mixed it with his rice and peas. Katie just watched.

He used his fork to scoop up a bit of rice and then stabbed a piece of chicken on the end. Katie just watched.

Halfway through chewing his first bite, he looked up at Katie staring at him. He swallowed and said, "Is something wrong?"

"I'm just shocked you aren't leaving me another note. I've gotten accustomed to spending the days and nights by myself. And apparently you're talking to me now, too?"

Katie was a little shocked at herself when she heard the words leave her mouth. But they were true.

Kyle didn't say a word. He just finished chewing.

"I'm sorry," Katie said. "It was just a long day." She ran both of her hands through her hair, feeling all the loose strands that had come undone from her ponytail. She looked down at her food. She was so frustrated she didn't want to eat, but she knew if she didn't she'd end up back at the cottage starving until breakfast.

Kyle set his fork on his plate and took a sip of his lemonade. "We haven't had a lot of guests since Hannah passed away."

She looked up. Kyle rested his forearms against the edge of the table as he spoke. "Hannah?" Katie said. "Doc accidentally called me that my first day here. I thought he'd just forgotten my name. Who is she?"

"She was Doc's wife."

"That's who Doc built the cottage for..." Katie said.

Kyle nodded.

Katie took a bite of her chicken. It was grilled and marinated in what tasted like Italian dressing. It was good.

"What was she like?"

Kyle smiled.

So he smiles, too.

"You would have liked her."

"How so?"

"She wasn't from around here."

"Where was she from?"

"Doc really doesn't like to talk about her all that much."

Of course he doesn't. Which I'm guessing means you're done talking about her. Figures.

Katie moved what was left of the chicken around on her plate. She had so many questions running through her mind now. She wanted answers about Hannah, but she could see that was a dead end, at least for tonight.

She tried another question. "What about your family? I mean, I know Doc is your uncle. But, what about your parents?"

Kyle put his fork and knife on his plate and walked it to the kitchen. "I'll be outside when you're done."

So, we can't talk about Hannah. You won't talk about your parents. And you'll talk about the dogs, but just not with me. Brilliant plan, Katie. Write a book about a bunch of dogs and the least talkative men on the planet.

Kyle walked Katie home in silence, keeping a few paces ahead of her the entire way.

She thought about trying to start another conversation, but she thought better of it. Her last question had hit a sore spot she could tell, and he obviously needed some space. So, when they arrived at the cottage Katie didn't even say goodnight. She just walked right past him and into the house. The solid white door closed behind her.

* * *

Kyle looked down at King, who was standing next to him. He shined the flashlight out in front of them a bit.

"That went better than last night, don't you think?"

King cocked his head sideways.

He sighed. "You're right. That didn't go well at all."

12

THE NEXT MORNING, Katie woke up without any more patience. Either Kyle would let her spend time with him while he trained the dogs and stop dodging her questions, or she would leave.

And maybe that's the point of it all. Maybe he wants it that way, she thought. How had she even made it five whole days in this place?

She didn't care. Today was Thursday, and her agent would be calling on Friday for an update. She hadn't spent most of the week doing chores in some barn for nothing. She needed her story, and the most she had so far were a myriad of descriptions about the few times she had seen the dogs—most of those about Belle or King.

Katie never got the chance to vent her frustration that morning, however. As soon as she reached the kitchen, it was clear that something wasn't right. Unlike previous mornings, there was no note stuffed in the door.

Katie looked around outside, under the mat, beneath the steps, even twenty or so feet in each direction from the house, thinking the wind may have somehow blown it away, though the trees were as calm as ever. There was no wind. In fact there was no sound at all. She didn't know what it was exactly, but something definitely felt wrong.

How is it that the one thing I've come to hate each morning is also the one thing I've counted on?

Without hesitation, she took off for the barn.

As she walked, she couldn't stop her mind from guessing what could be wrong.

Is one of the dogs hurt?

She walked faster.

Has something happened to Doc?

She began to jog.

Is Kyle okay?

She broke into a run.

Moments later, Katie reached the barn nearly out of breath. She looked into the barn, but Kyle wasn't there. A second later, she heard the familiar squeak of the screen door opening and she saw Kyle exiting Doc's house. For a moment she smiled, mostly in relief at the realization that he was fine. Maybe she had finally earned his trust and there weren't going to be any more stupid chores.

Her smile quickly faded.

His demeanor seemed as collected as always, but when he looked at her she noticed the calm in his eyes was gone. He didn't say a single word, but kept walking past her towards the barn.

And then she saw his hands.

He was carrying one of the steel toolboxes that held medical supplies for the dogs—the same ones she'd cleaned out earlier this week. But what alarmed her were the red stains that streaked down each forearm. What alarmed her was the blood.

Katie quickly scanned the empty lot near the house, where Doc parked his truck. It wasn't there. *Figures.* Before she knew it, her legs were moving as she followed Kyle into the barn.

"Kyle," she called after him.

He didn't stop walking, but yelled over his shoulder. "Not now, Miss Price."

Katie jogged after him anyway.

He turned abruptly to face her. She almost ran right into him. The look in his eyes was like a heavy weight pressing down on her.

"Kyle, what's wrong?"

As much as he may not have wanted her there, she could tell from the look in his eye that he needed her help. "I don't have time to explain. But if you are going to stay, you need to do exactly as I say. Understood?"

Katie didn't say a word, just nodded and followed Kyle to the other end of the barn, where Belle lay dying.

13

FOR WHAT IT WAS WORTH, Katie tried to listen to Kyle. She tried to follow his detailed instructions, each one crafted as if today her note was simply verbal, not written. But from the moment she saw Belle, she froze.

The dog lay in the corner of the stall near the same recessed hole that Katie had seen her in for the past few days. Only this time, Belle looked different. She lay on her side, breathing hard. White foam had formed around her lips. She tried to lift her head off the dirt floor to look towards Katie, but Kyle gently pushed it back down.

"Calm, girl. Calm."

His voice broke her trance and Katie knelt next to Kyle. "What's wrong with her?"

Kyle didn't respond. "There's another black medical bag on top of the bench, by the tools," he said, motioning to the other end of the barn. She knew exactly where it was, since she was the one who'd put it there.

Katie stood immediately, but before she could turn she saw something lying just a few feet from Belle. There were three small, dark objects curled up in the hay. Motionless. She took a step forward and suddenly realized what they were. Puppies.

She had never seen puppies so small in her entire life. Curled up that way, they could easily fit in one of her hands.

"Are they..." Katie started, but Kyle cut her off.

"The bag. Now."

Katie came running back with the bag seconds later. Kyle was still on his hands and knees. He had pulled on a pair of latex gloves and felt softly up and down Belle's side.

Kyle immediately unlatched the bag as Katie set it down. He handed her a bottle of antiseptic surgical hand wash. "Wash both hands and put these on," he said, passing her a pair of clear latex gloves.

By the time she'd finished, he had pulled out what looked like a small turkey baster and several towels. He looked at her intently and spoke slow and clear. "Belle was not able to clean the first three pups. Wipe them down gently with a little bit of water and the towels. Check their noses and mouths for any excess placenta. If they're showing any difficulty breathing, use the small suction tube to clear the airways."

Katie nodded her head in understanding, but she didn't move.

"Do it now."

It took less than two minutes to check the pups. They were cleaned and appeared to be breathing normally, every now and then making small subtle movements in the hay. Katie breathed a sigh of relief. But as she turned back to Kyle, she knew there were still problems with Belle.

Kyle had lifted Belle's tail and was applying some type of clear gel-like substance.

Katie knelt beside him, leaving the puppies to wriggle in the hay several feet from her. She looked down at Belle and stroked the patch of tan fur above her eyes.

"It's okay, Belle. Your puppies are okay. You're going to be okay."

But as Katie ran her hand several more times over Belle's soft fur, she realized something was very wrong. Belle wasn't panting anymore.

Katie leaned in closer to her mouth, but she heard nothing. Belle was not breathing.

"I need you to keep talking to her, Miss Price. Keep her calm."

"She's not breathing," Katie said urgently. She turned to Kyle and inadvertently grabbed his shoulder. "Kyle, I don't think she's breathing."

Kyle ignored her for a moment. He had placed a small flashlight in his mouth and was looking just below Belle's tail.

Katie turned her head sideways and placed her ear close to Belle's mouth again. No sound. She barely noticed the tears streaming down her own face. The only friend she'd had over the last few days now lay motionless in front of her. This was not the kind of story Katie wanted. Then, two large hands wrapped themselves around her shoulders and Doc lifted her to her feet.

It all felt like it was happening so slowly. Like everything was still, when it should be chaotic. People should be running around frantically like they did in the movies when someone was rushed to the emergency room. But in front of her were just two men. There was no army of doctors. No fancy machines beeping out signals and information. Just two men.

And then, suddenly it was like someone had flipped a switch and the world around her was moving faster than she could keep up with.

The last puppy had breached during birth. Usually a puppy would be born tail first or head first, but the fourth—and final puppy—was facing head first with both of its paws pushed forward. Katie later learned this wasn't uncommon, but had caused dystocia. Basically, Belle couldn't push the puppy out during birth because of its position in the birth canal.

When Doc arrived, after he had pulled Katie to the side, he lifted Belle's tail and pulled the puppy out in a matter of seconds. He cut the umbilical cord and cleaned it just as Kyle had instructed Katie, and then sat it with the others. It was fine.

What happened next was nothing short of a miracle.

Kyle had done everything with such care earlier, but once the puppy was out Katie noticed an increased urgency in his movements. He pushed Belle onto her right side and pressed two fingers about halfway up the inside of her left hind leg.

He quickly moved around to the front side of Belle and straightened her body so her neck wasn't bent up. Then he leaned in closely.

"I've got a pulse, but she's not breathing," he said to Doc, the tension audible in his voice.

He moved to Belle's mouth, opened it, and pulled her tongue forward, looking to clear anything that might be obstructing her airway. There was nothing. He moved one hand under the lower jaw and closed it, placing the thumb of the same hand on top of the muzzle to keep the mouth shut. He cupped his other hand around the muzzle and placed his mouth over the dog's nose and mouth and blew several quick breaths. He paused and Doc pressed several times on Belle's stomach, allowing the air to exhale, and then repeated.

What actually took seconds, felt like hours to Katie. And then he stopped.

Katie rushed back over, frantic. "Why are you stopping? You can't give up—you can't."

Doc tried to calm her, but it wasn't until Kyle said her name that she actually heard anything.

"Katie," Kyle said. He took her hand and placed it on Belle's stomach. Katie felt the gentle rise and fall of the dog's breathing. "Belle is going to be fine."

14

KATIE SAT ON THE BARN FLOOR, her knees pulled up to her chest, her back against one of the timber poles as she watched Kyle. He inspected each puppy thoroughly, as Doc continued to monitor Belle's vitals off and on for several hours. There was a small leather-bound notebook tucked away inside the medical box. Kyle gave each puppy a separate page and recorded their temperatures, weight, colors, length, and so on.

He checked their heart rate, inspected their mouths and noses as much as possible, gently toweled them off one last time, and then encouraged them to nurse by placing them close to Belle. Kyle spoke to Katie as he worked through the exercises, explaining what he was doing.

"Nose, eyes, ears," Kyle said as he put the notebook back in the box and walked over to Katie. He knelt down in front of her and held his hand towards her, palm down.

Katie wiped her eyes and tucked a few strands of hair behind her ears. The intimacy of his movement surprised her—up until now, it seemed Kyle went out of his way to avoid her as much as possible. "What does that mean?"

"It's how you greet a dog. They're born with only a sense of smell and touch. They can't open their eyes for seven to ten days, and then their ears won't start fully functioning until around fifteen days. They're brought into the world in a specific order. They smell their mother, they see their mother, and then they hear their mother. But when most people greet dogs you'll notice they make eye contact, say something, and reach for the animal. The dog may respond, but ultimately this type of greeting may startle a pup. When you greet any of the dogs here I want you to remember 'nose, eyes, ears.'"

Katie nodded and forced a smile as Kyle finished cleaning up. *Lot of good that's going to do, since you don't even let me around the dogs.*

Her eyes were red and itchy from crying, and she felt foolish for breaking down. After several more minutes, she finally stood and went to Belle's stall, resting her forearms on the top board. Doc was kneeling beside Belle with a stethoscope, gently moving it around her body as she breathed. The puppies lay nearly motionless, except for the subtle rise and fall of their chests as they slept. Occasionally, one of them would twitch.

"Are they dreaming?" Katie asked, motioning towards one of the puppy's legs as it extended and pulled back quickly several times.

"It is possible," Doc replied. "But, not probable."

"What do you mean?"

"Well, what would they be dreaming about?"

Katie thought about it for a moment. She recalled what Kyle had said about their eyes and ears not even being opened yet.

"I…I'm not sure."

85

Doc tucked the stethoscope back in the black medical bag and shifted his weight to his other knee so he was crouched in front of the puppies. He pointed to the puppy's leg that was twitching slightly. "These are like brand new bodies for these little guys. They've been cooped up inside their momma for several months and their muscles aren't developed. So, they subconsciously twitch and shake in their sleep. But what they're really doing is preparing their bodies to walk, and crawl, and scratch, and what have you."

"That's actually kind of amazing."

"Yes, indeed it is."

Katie watched Doc for several more minutes and realized where Kyle's attention to detail came from. His hands moved with a natural precision as he re-packed the medical bag with the last of his tools and gently patted Belle on her side.

He groaned slightly as he stood, rubbing the joint around his left knee, and broke the silence that resonated through the barn. Katie looked around for Kyle as Doc closed the door to Belle's pen, but he was still out with a few of the dogs. She turned back to Belle. "It's just you and me, girl. Don't worry, I'm not going anywhere for a while."

15

KYLE FINISHED WITH THE DOGS for the day and walked over to his work bench, which sat a few feet into the barn. The late-afternoon sun cast his shadow lengthwise down the barn floor, where he saw Katie sitting in front of Belle's pen. She was turned to the side looking in on Belle.

He was surprised to still see her there, especially sitting on the ground. He figured she'd have headed back to the cottage for a shower before dinner. She always smelled of lavender when they sat down to eat, something he had come to like.

She must have heard him enter the barn or toss the broken harness on the table, but if she did, she made no sign of it.

He lifted the two latches on his Craftsman toolbox and opened and slid out the third tray. He pulled out a pair of needle-nose pliers and shut the drawer, looking back down towards Katie. She still hadn't even looked over his way. He noticed her sweater was caught on a splinter in the timber, revealing her trim, tanned back.

Looking back at the harness on the table, he realized he'd forgotten what he'd come in here to do. He stared down at the harness, an old x-back. His eyes followed the curving lines of the nylon webbing, but his mind was still focused on Katie.

It was odd seeing her sit so quietly. Usually she'd be with her computer, or in the corner with her notebook. Or asking him a thousand pointless questions. *I don't understand why Doc let her stay here. She's not going to learn anything.* Even as he thought the words, though, he realized they weren't true. To be honest, it was nice to see her like this—sitting with Belle for no reason related to her story. Just kind of being a part of things. Wasn't this what he had tried to tell her from the beginning?

His eyes continued tracing along the harness until they landed on a silver latch ring that had torn through the material. Flipping the harness over, he saw that the seam had ripped through the backside. There was no way to fix this.

He put the pliers back in the toolbox, shut the tray firmly, and flipped down both latches. Katie had hardly moved. Before he could stop himself, he walked towards her. *I can't believe I'm doing this. It's like an invitation for more questions.*

"She looks good," Kyle said, the dirt and hay crunching lightly under his boots as he stopped next to Belle's pen. He rested his arms on the top board, and looked down at Belle.

"She's worried," Katie said.

He looked at her, surprised. "Worried?"

"Yeah. She's worried about Hope."

"Hope?"

"Well, you didn't tell me her name, so that's what I've been calling her," Katie said. She motioned to the puppy curled up by Belle's neck. The same one that had caused the complications earlier today.

Kyle smiled.

"Why is that so funny?" she said with a serious expression.

"I'm not laughing."

"Then what are you…"

Kyle interrupted her. "I'm just happy that you're finally starting to see the dogs."

16

KYLE FINISHED CLEANING UP near his work bench and exited the barn towards the house. Katie watched as he left, leaving her to a moonlit barn full of dogs. She stood up and stretched her legs for the first time in a couple hours, brushing a few pieces of loose hay off the back of her jeans. Dinner would be ready soon, and she'd have to leave Belle.

The barn door creaked and Katie turned to see Kyle sliding it shut. She took that as a hint that it was time to leave.

"Don't worry, girl, I'll be back in the morning," Katie whispered. But as Katie turned to leave she saw Kyle walking towards her carrying a large basket.

When he reached her, he set the basket down and unfolded a large gray towel in front of Belle's pen.

Katie stood silently and watched as he unpacked two plates covered in tinfoil, a thermos, some silverware, and two glasses.

When he was finished arranging everything he poured the two glasses full of water and sat down on the towel, his back leaning against Belle's pen and his feet stretched out in front of him.

Kyle started to peel back the foil on his plate and looked up at Katie still standing there. "Aren't you hungry?"

"Did you just make me a picnic?"

Kyle folded the tinfoil twice into a square and set it back in the basket. "Do they not have picnics in California?"

He looked right at her as he asked, holding her gaze. *Why is he is so hard to read?*

"Of course we have picnics." She sat down on the towel next to her plate of food. "I've just never been on one," she said under her breath. She pulled the foil off her plate and started to crumble it into a little ball, but stopped and instead folded it neatly as she had watched Kyle do.

Underneath the foil sat a considerable portion of baked beans alongside a large cheeseburger. The sauce from the baked beans was inching towards the burger. Katie moved the burger towards the side of her plate and pulled off the top bun. There was lettuce, what looked and smelled like Thousand Island dressing, and a dark orange cheese with red flecks.

"Pimiento cheese," Kyle said.

"What?"

"The orange stuff you're staring at. It's pimiento cheese. It's good southern food."

Katie looked back at Kyle.

"Trust me."

She picked up her burger and took a huge bite. The cool lettuce crunched against the warm meat and a mixture of the dressing and cheese spilled out the side of the bun and back onto her plate.

As she began to chew, a piece of lettuce fell out of her mouth. She turned to pick it up off her jeans and found Kyle grinning at her. "What?" she tried to say with a full mouth.

"Sometimes you surprise me," he said.

Katie finished chewing. "How so?"

Before Kyle could answer, King came trotting in. He sniffed around Katie's feet and then laid down next to Kyle.

Katie watched King as the dog laid his head across Kyle's feet. Then she looked around at some of the other dogs watching from their pen. Dixie was sitting directly across the barn with her pitch-black head and amber eyes resting on the toe board of her pen. Spirit was in the adjacent pen, one of her white paws draped over a board, also silently staring back at Katie.

"Will you tell me something about the dogs?" Katie asked.

Kyle scooped up a forkful of baked beans, poured them over the edge of his burger, and took a bite.

From behind her Katie heard the familiar rustle of hay, as Belle shifted her weight over her makeshift paillasse. Shards and bits of stems and leaves poked through the cloth sack.

"Often times when a person looks at a dog they forget that the dog doesn't look back at them the same way."

"What do you mean?"

Kyle looked over at Dixie, still laying at the front of the pen. He motioned with his hand. "When she sees you she doesn't see a pretty brunette girl that loves to write."

Katie blushed, and tried to focus on something other than the fact that he just called he pretty.

"She sees the way your shoulders are slightly angled towards her. She notices the few strands of hair not tucked behind your ear. She watches the subtle part in your lips.

"The dogs see everything. The way you walk, the lightness or heaviness of a single step. The way you look at things, with curiosity or insecurity. Even the way you breathe. They take the time to notice the details that we often take for granted. All their decisions are based on these details."

Kyle took another bite of his burger and fell back into the silence that defined him.

Katie watched the dogs as they ate, with an awareness she hadn't known before. She was attentive to every shift in their stance, every twitching ear. The softness of their eyes.

Kyle sat near enough that she could feel his warmth, though they didn't touch. She found it enough, somehow, just to sit with him.

Kyle waited for her to finish and gathered everything except the towel Katie was still sitting on and placed it back in the basket.

Kyle looked down at King still lying there. "Let me just run this inside and we'll walk you back to the cottage."

As Kyle walked out of the barn she watched him the same way the dogs had watched her. She noticed the lightness in his steps, how the back left of his shirt was tucked slightly into his jeans, and the tightness of his shirt around his shoulders. She couldn't help but wonder if he always looked at her that way.

17

WHEN KATIE FINALLY REACHED the cottage that night, she didn't even make it to the bedroom. Instead, she sat down at the first chair she reached. She was exhausted. Completely drained from the hours spent with Belle and the newborn puppies.

But her mind was also racing from Kyle's words.

Contrary to what most people think, Katie had learned that the majority of the time when a writer sits down to write, it's systematic, not inspirational. She'd learned this from her father at an early age— writing was a routine, and in that routine she could open a door that led to a journey she'd never expect.

As Katie sat there staring at the pad and pencil on the kitchen counter, she knew her experience today could be the key to one of those doors.

She wrote like she needed to write, and as her fingers pressed against the cool keyboard she recalled a poem by Richard Wilbur that her father used to love.

In her room at the prow of the house
Where light breaks, and the windows are tossed with linden,
My daughter is writing a story...

And so Katie wrote like the young girl at the typewriter, as if it was a matter of life and death. With moments of inspiration and frustration. But never ceasing. Her light on all night long. The words spilled onto the page as if they had been bottled up for too long and needed to get out. Until finally, she collapsed in sheer exhaustion at the table.

* * *

A loud chirping noise woke Katie from her sleep. It was a noise she hadn't heard in nearly a week.

She looked down at the phone buzzing next to her computer and quickly tried to rub the sleep from her eyes.

"Why are you calling me so early?" Katie grumbled into the phone.

"Please tell me you have something," Sam pleaded.

Katie opened her laptop, which she'd used as a pillow most of the night, and stared at the words in front of her.

She let out a sigh of relief. "I do," she said, half-smiling, half-squinting as the morning light poured into the cottage.

"You do?" Sam asked again, incredulous.

"I do."

"Well, it's about time. And by the way, what do you mean by early? It's almost noon where you are."

It took a moment for those words to set in. *It's almost noon.* "Shoot, I've gotta run. I'll send you the draft as soon as I can."

Before Sam could say bye Katie ended the call, set the phone on the table, and took off towards the shower.

Noon! How could it possibly be that late! How late did I stay up writing?

She was glad to have written enough to keep her agent satisfied, but she still needed to spend actual time with Kyle and the dogs. She had a story, but she still needed the magic behind it.

After a quick shower, she threw on a pair of jeans and a white t-shirt, and grabbed her backpack with her laptop and a sweater stuffed inside.

But as she stepped out the front door, she couldn't help but shake the feeling that she was missing something. Then it hit her. For the second day in a row there was no note on the door.

Was something wrong again? Was Belle okay?

She couldn't help but think something terrible had happened overnight. She knew she shouldn't have listened to Kyle and returned to the cottage—she should have stayed with Belle.

When she reached the house, she found Kyle and Doc on the front porch sipping coffee. Biscuit lay at Doc's feet while her litter roughhoused with each other in the dirt at the bottom of the steps. They were all there: Saint, Solomon, Samson, Rev, and Angel.

Katie surprised herself with how easily she recalled their names. She could picture the hand-carved wooden boards hanging from their pen.

She jogged up the steps, past the dogs, and walked directly over to Kyle.

"You scared me half to death!" she scolded him.

Appearing confused and a little surprised at her tone, Kyle didn't say a word.

"This is the second day in a row that you didn't leave a note. And after what happened last night, I thought something was wrong. Which, obviously it's not."

"Didn't you tell me the night before that you hate those notes?"

"I did. I do, but..."

From the corner of her eye she could see a smile spread across Doc's face as he took another sip of his coffee.

"This is not funny," Katie said as she turned to Doc.

But she couldn't help but smile as Doc started to laugh.

"It's not funny!" she tried to force a serious tone.

"Okay, okay. Kyle, you owe Miss Price an apology."

Kyle looked at Doc with a blank expression and then got up and walked right past Katie, down the front steps, and towards the barn.

Before Katie could react, Kyle stopped and looked over his shoulder. "I thought you wanted to spend some time with the dogs?"

Katie tried to feign a serious expression, but her face lit up. "This better not be some ploy where I walk into the barn and you hand me another shovel and a bucket."

"That's a risk you'll just have to take."

Katie looked back at Kyle as he stood there waiting for her response. He was wearing a long-sleeved crewneck shirt the color of beach sand. The end of his sleeves were frayed and there were several small holes around the hem of his collar. She couldn't think of anything except how the fabric of his shirt was tighter around his chest.

"You could always stay with Doc. I think he's making some homemade dog manure for his tomatoes."

"Don't you go putting me in the middle of this," Doc said between sips of coffee.

Of course she wanted to go, but the phone call with her agent that morning tugged at her.

"Of all days, you had to pick today."

Kyle looked up towards the cloudless sky. "Today looks like a good day to me."

Katie agreed. It was a gorgeous day. She looked down at her backpack, where her laptop lay in wait. "I need to run into town to send something to my agent. Unless," Katie turned back to Doc," you have access to the internet here?"

Doc shook his said. "Sorry, milady, we do not. But, I believe Kyle can help you out with that."

Katie was a little confused. "You have internet...in...the...barn?"

Kyle gave a slight grin and shook his head. "No, but I know a place that does."

18

KYLE POLITELY ASKED KATIE to wait outside the barn as he got the dogs ready. She had seen all the dogs a lot over the past few days, but her only real interaction had been with King and Belle, other than the puppies. She thought Kyle might still be worried about how the dogs would react to her.

"Miss Price," he called from the cover of the barn, gesturing her inside with a nod of his head.

I thought we were finally over this Miss Price thing…

Katie took several steps forward, into the shadow of the barn.

Sitting perfectly still in front of their pens were fourteen dogs. As she looked around, Katie realized that each of the dogs were mostly paired together—one older dog and one pup around eight months old, from the previous litter.

Directly in front of her was some type of makeshift wooden wagon, except on the backside was a hollow steel handle that rose about four feet above the base. There were four spoke wheels, and what looked like two small pedestals or footholds in the back, as well.

What was most odd wasn't the vehicle itself, but the harnesses that were attached to the front. There were fifteen individual harnesses, fourteen of which were paired together, with a single harness at the lead.

That's when Katie realized this wasn't a wagon at all, but a sled.

"Coming, Miss Price?" Kyle said with a hint of a smile.

Katie thought back to the first day she'd been at the farm, watching Kyle train the dogs in pairs. He had been training them to work as a team.

All this time he had been training them to become…sled dogs? Who trained sled dogs in South Carolina?

"I don't understand," Katie said.

Kyle walked over to Katie and held out his hand, palm up, as if he were a chauffeur. She took it and he helped her step up onto the sled, which was nothing more than a piece of plywood about two feet wide and four feet long, with one-inch-by-six-inch timbers lining the sides. It was more or less a box on wheels.

Katie stepped in and sat cross-legged with her bag in her lap as Kyle began to check all lines attached to the sled.

"I still don't understand," she said again. "You train sled dogs?"

Kyle walked to the front of the sled and tugged lightly on the center line that was attached to the sled. He didn't answer her question, but began explaining instead.

"There are four lines, all of which are referred to as rigging," he began, grasping the center line and holding it off the ground. "You should be familiar; you've been cleaning and sorting it for the past few days," he said with a grin.

Katie looked down at the nylon lines. He was right. She had just assumed they were used for some type of training.

How did I not see this sooner?

"This is the tow line, and it connects to the bridle," he said, pointing to two short lines connected to the front left and front right of the sled. "It also connects to this safety line or shock line. It's more or less a backup line in case the tow line was to snap."

Katie unzipped her bag as slowly and quietly as possible, pulling out her notepad and pencil as Kyle continued.

He spoke in such great detail, explaining the intricacies of each line all the way down to the different types of threads. She had no clue what he was talking about half the time, but she kept writing anyway. She was just grateful he was talking to her at all considering the rough start they'd had, let alone carving out the details of the story she had been trying to capture for almost a week.

Kyle stopped examining the rigging and stood tall next to the front of the sled. "Colossus. Come."

Katie looked up from writing. In the field and the barn, Kyle communicated with the dogs mostly with hand gestures. This was only the second time she'd ever heard him speak to the dogs. His tone was different with the dogs than with her. There was no hesitation.

Katie turned her eyes from Kyle and towards the black and tan dog that moved towards him. Colossus was one of the first dogs she could recall seeing that day in the field. He was huge—the only dog she'd seen that was larger than King. As he trotted over this time, she noticed his tail was more downturned than the other dogs, and his hind legs were thick and powerful.

Kyle slipped a harness on Colossus, buckling it over the top of his back, and connected two lines to him: one to his collar—the neck line—and one to his harness—the tug line. When he was finished, Kyle called the next dog.

"Olympia. Come."

Olympia was in direct contrast to Colossus. Her coat was entirely ginger and she glided gracefully over to Kyle. She was large, but she wasn't quite the size of Colossus.

Kyle hooked her into the lines the same way he had Colossus. Both dogs stood side by side, directly in front of the sled.

"All the dogs out here are very strong. But Colossus and Olympia are wheel dogs—they're not only responsible for the initial weight of the sled, but they're also two of the most even-tempered dogs. Which is necessary when we take steep hills or declines and the sled is constantly slamming against the ground. While some dogs may be distracted or unnerved by this, good wheel dogs aren't."

Kyle turned back to the remaining twelve dogs and continued.

Giza and Gardens were next, followed by Artemis, Alexandria, Hali, Sunshine, Boone, Wyatt, Raley, and Raggles.

Giza and Gardens looked similar to Colossus in color, but were both female. They walked with ease and grace when Kyle called them. Artemis was one of the oldest dogs in the pack at twelve years, while Alexandria was just shy of one. Hali was a dark rich black, while Sunshine was mostly white with black spots that looked like clouds. Boone and Wyatt were the other two ginger coats on the team. For some reason the fur on top of Boone's head was always puffed up, and Katie couldn't help but smile. Raley and Raggles were of similar age, though

Raley must have been sneaking extra treats because he looked to be ten pounds heavier than Raggles.

Kyle paused after he had hooked them in, and Katie was surprised at how much she had remembered about each of the dogs. "These are the team dogs. They're the fuel of the sled. Colossus and Olympia may *get* them going, but the team *keeps* them going."

Only two dogs remained.

"Story. Link. Come."

These were the only two dogs that Kyle had called together. They were also the only two that shared a pen, and the same two that Katie remembered Kyle with in the field. While Colossus and Olympia were a contrast in appearance, Story and Link were a complete contrast in personality. Link was several years older than Story, and his demeanor mirrored that. His stride was slow and his eyes were calm. Story, on the other hand, was the picture of energy and exuberance. From the moment Kyle spoke her name she jolted into action, playfully growling as she literally ran into Link's side, eliciting laughs from both Katie and Kyle.

Kyle took a second to calm Story and said, "These are the swing dogs. When the team turns together, it's because of them. They have to be more alert and aware than the team and wheel dogs. They must be incredibly quick, not only with their feet, but with their minds as well."

All fourteen dogs stood patiently in front of the sled—except Story, who was nipping at Link's feet. If Link was bothered, he didn't show it. Instead, his eyes followed the erratic path of a horsefly buzzing around the barn.

Katie closed her notebook and slid her pencil between the spiral binding. She massaged her hand, now aching from furiously taking notes, and looked down at the dogs in front of her.

Was she really sitting in a makeshift sled—or a "basket," as Kyle had explained was the proper name—in the middle of South Carolina, harnessed to fourteen dogs? It almost didn't seem real.

She looked back at some of the other dogs still sitting in their pens. Dixie, Jade, Maynard, Mingo, Shyanne, and Spirit looked back at her. Belle and her pups were resting peacefully, but the other dogs looked disappointed that they hadn't been chosen.

Her eyes turned to follow Kyle as he made his way from dog to dog, checking each rigging line and connection for any faults. A light gust of wind swept through the barn and moved something that caught her attention. She looked towards the front of the sled, where one harness lay empty on the ground.

Katie's knowledge of dog sledding only stretched as far as the explanations Kyle had been giving for the past ten minutes. But it only took a little bit of common sense to understand the lead dog was missing.

"Are you missing one dog still?" Katie asked.

Kyle didn't respond, which Katie was used to. She was beginning to think he did it on purpose, just to bother her. Instead, he walked towards the front of the team and placed both of his pinky fingers in his mouth. It was a series of high-low-high whistles that he repeated several times, the tone floating across the barn and over the land. Kyle knelt down near the lead harness after a few seconds, but nothing happened.

Several of the dogs' ears began to press down against their necks. Their tails flattened. Story's demeanor changed entirely, as she went from biting at Link's feet to standing alert. She sniffed the air around her as her ears moved independently, locating the sound she heard making its way towards them.

A split second later, King broke Katie's line of sight. He entered at the far end of the barn, mouth closed, ears standing straight up, and tail curled over his back. He moved towards Kyle with a steady gait, but Katie felt as if he never took his eyes off her.

As Kyle placed the harness around King, Katie was surprised that he would be the lead dog. He spent no time training with the others. In fact, since she had been here he had spent a considerable portion of his time just watching her.

Kyle whispered something to King before he stood, and walked to the back of the sled. He stepped up onto the footboards directly behind Katie. "Line out!"

Kyle's voice startled her as it carried through the barn.

King reacted immediately. He took several steps forward, pulling the tow line taut.

Katie turned around slightly and looked up towards Kyle. "I appreciate everything you've done. Really. But, I have to get something sent to my agent by noon. And I need internet access to do that."

"Yes, you mentioned that about ten minutes ago."

"Okay. So you have internet somewhere on the farm?" Katie asked, somewhat confused.

"No."

"But..." she offered, hoping he was going to complete that thought.

"I'm not taking you somewhere on the farm."

"Then where are we going?"

"Friday is food day. We're going to town."

"On a sled?"

Kyle didn't respond.

"Wait. I thought you and Doc told me the closest town was Camden or Florence, which is almost an hour away."

"No. Doc told you the closest *city* was Camden or Florence. The closest *town* is the one we're on the outskirts of right now. And it's about a half-hour away. That is, if we ever actually leave."

"And there's internet there?"

King let out a groan from the front of the pack.

"I know," Kyle said. "I told you she was difficult."

Katie sighed. "You know, you could have just told me all of this from the beginning."

"You could have just trusted me."

Katie rolled her eyes and mumbled under her breath as she turned back around. "Yeah, because you've given me so many reasons to.

"So, do I just sit here?" she asked more loudly.

"Hike!" Kyle yelled.

She jolted back against the sled rails, lightly banging her shoulder, and dropped her notebook as King and the other dogs propelled the sled into motion.

"And hold on," Kyle added with a grin.

19

THIRTY MINUTES LATER, King halted the pack without Kyle's command, about twenty feet from a long row of wooden fence that lined the road.

The ride had been a little bumpy, but more than worth it.

Once they had lost sight of the barn, the dogs found their rhythm. Each pair had a purpose, Kyle had explained on the way.

Katie loved watching each of the dogs, but mostly she watched King. He was older, but he was strong and steadfast. She noticed the gait of several of the younger dogs change as they went over a small hill or through a thick patch of grass. But King made the change in pace several yards in advance, and the older dogs followed suit.

Kyle had to correct the younger ones verbally at each fault, which was something Katie also found that she came to like. She had not seem him interact much with the dogs verbally, but from the sled all the dogs were in front of him and hand signals couldn't be used.

As Kyle stepped off the back of the sled, the dogs instantly relaxed. They were already panting, but some sat or laid in the cool grass.

There was a wooden box the width of the sled behind where Katie was sitting, and as she got up Kyle opened the lid and pulled out eight plastic bowls and two bottles of water. He put one bowl in front of each pair and poured a quarter of the bottle in each bowl.

Placing the empty bottles back in the box, he pulled out one more full bottle.

He turned to Katie and extended the bottle in her direction.

"No, thank you," she said as she brushed the dirt from the sled off her jeans.

Kyle walked quickly over to King and unhooked his harness, then shook the bottle several times in front of the dog.

King sat as Kyle poured the water from the bottle, slowly enough that it almost looked like King was drinking water like a human. Katie looked around at the myriad of wildflowers that adorned the straw-like grass. There were bright yellow daisies, deep red poppies, bits of baby's breath, and other blues and oranges she didn't recognize. They were almost to the edge of the property, where Katie hadn't been before.

Kyle refilled a few more bowls, pushed a small latch into the ground behind one of the tires—which Katie assumed was some type of brake—and turned to Katie. "Ready?"

"We're just going to leave all the dogs here?"

"No."

"They're coming with us to the store?"

"No."

Katie looked at Kyle with the same look she'd given him earlier in the barn. As they walked, Katie asked the question that had gone unanswered earlier in the barn.

"Kyle," Katie said, stopping several steps behind him. "I still don't understand. I get that you train sled dogs, but it just doesn't make any sense. Aren't sled dogs supposed to be huskies? Don't they need to be training in zero-degree weather up in Canada or Alaska or something? Are you from up north? How do you know how to train dogs for this? Where do these dogs even come from?"

Her questions came out rapid-fire. She had so many coursing through her mind. At first they'd just been the questions of an inquisitive writer looking for answers, but now they felt like much more.

Kyle stopped at the base of a small hill. The sound of a car driving by interrupted the silence and Katie realized they must be close to town.

"That's a lot of questions," Kyle said, continuing up the hill.

"I'm sorry. I've been wanting to ask you, but it never seems like the right time. You're always busy and you've got me running around all day doing chores. Even at dinner you hardly let on about the dogs at all.

"Sometimes there never is a right time," Kyle offered.

"Don't you want people to know about the dogs? I can share their story in your own words if you'd let me."

When they reached the top of the hill, he stopped again and turned to face Katie. "The Siberian husky, the Alaskan husky, the Samoyed, the Canadian Eskimo, the Chinook, the Alaskan malamute. They are all incredible dogs. Intelligent, hardworking, fierce. They make great sled dogs and great sled dog teams." Kyle hesitated as he looked directly into Katie's eyes. "But, they will never match a Carolina gray.

"Colder climates would help some, but they don't matter a whole lot. And as far as where these dogs come from," he said motioning at King, "you should do some research on the Jindo, the Beringia, the Carolina dog, and the gray wolf." He looked over at Katie and laughed. "I can't be doing all the work now."

Katie pressed Kyle. "I can appreciate that, and I will definitely look into all of it. But I'm not looking for the origin of the dogs, as much as I am the origin of your story with the dogs."

Kyle was silent for a few seconds as they continued walking. Something moved near the trees off to the right, and King trotted towards it.

I don't understand, Katie thought. *Why is everything such a mystery with him? Am I still just some stranger that he doesn't want to talk to?*

"I was just a boy at the time," Kyle began. "It was a soft sound, barely audible. And for a moment I almost ignored it. But then I heard it again. Still trying to catch my breath, I took several steps into the woods. Lying on the ground was a black wolf. Or so I thought..."

Kyle stopped walking and turned towards Katie—towards the land that Doc owned. "Years ago, hunters had laid traps all through these lands," he said, motioning with his hands. "Doc had spent months trying to find them all, but he must have missed one. The animal lay motionless on its side, the steel trap clamped around its back paw, blood and fur matted together. At first I thought it was dead, but when I moved it jolted up, straining against the trap. She screamed like nothing

I had ever heard before. It sounded no different than a human screaming out in pain—but that wasn't the sound I had heard moments before. From behind the wolf, a small black shape moved. A pup.

"When I returned with Doc, he wouldn't let me near the animal. He had his rifle in hand and told me there was no other choice. I was kicking and screaming for him not to shoot it. I don't know why, just something went off inside of me. I ran several steps in front of her and stopped, holding my arms out to protect it."

Katie listened intently, picturing the story as he told it. She imagined him as a young boy—his hair lighter, but his eyes just as brown. She could all but see him standing in front of the wounded animal. Protective, just as he still is.

"I don't remember what happened next because it all happened so fast. One moment I was standing in front of the wolf, the next Doc was kneeling beside it, prying the trap apart. I had thoughts of Doc freeing the animal and nursing it back to health, but the moment he opened the trap the wolf darted off. Leaving the pup behind." Kyle pointed at King, who was trotting back towards them.

"So, is King a wolf?" Katie asked.

"For the first few years of his life I still thought I was raising a wolf. That is, until one day a man from the University of Georgia showed up. His name was Dr. Behr Lisbon, and he was an ecologist studying wildlife around the Savannah River. A lot of people get lost around these parts, so when he pulled up I just assumed Doc would be giving him directions and he'd be back on his way. But when he stepped out of the car, a dark gray wolf followed. For a moment, I honestly believed it was King's mother."

Unable to contain herself Katie quickly asked, "Was it?"

Kyle looked up at the sky, and shielded his eyes. The sun was almost directly overhead. "I thought you had something important to do by noon?"

"Seriously?"

"Seriously."

"*Seriously?*"

"Is this some game people play out in California?"

Katie laughed. "You know what I'm asking. Was it King's mother?"

"Unfortunately not."

"And...?" Katie said, motioning for him to go on.

"And, I suggest you talk to Dr. Lisbon at some point. He discovered a new breed of wild dogs in the area—which he called Carolina dogs—that travelled in packs with similar characteristics to a dingo."

"But Earl said your dogs were part wolf."

Kyle nodded. "My dogs are what I call Carolina grays. They are Carolina dogs that bred with gray wolves years and years ago."

"What about you?" Katie asked. She regretted the question as soon as she asked it. She was prying again and she knew it. At the same time, though, she couldn't help herself.

Kyle looked down at King trotting between him and Katie. Then he looked directly at Katie and she saw the same hesitation in his eyes that she'd seen that night at dinner.

What is he hiding?

It seemed to Katie that there were stories he'd locked away somewhere—stories he couldn't bring himself to share. He shrugged as he ducked between the top and bottom rail of the wooden fence with King following.

Just across the street Katie saw a familiar wooden sign that read "Pearl's Place."

20

KYLE REACHED THE DOOR FIRST, and held it open for Katie. "We'll be back in a bit," he said to King. "Stay."

The door shut behind him and Katie asked, "Will he be okay?"

Before Kyle could respond, Katie heard a familiar voice. "You better not be trackin' any dirt in here."

"Good afternoon to you too, Miss Pearl," Kyle said.

Pearl turned around from behind the far end of the counter, where she had been restocking the shelves with large brown bags of what looked like sugar. She wiped her hands on her apron and walked over to Kyle. "What can I do you for today?" Pearl said.

"Three dozen eggs, a pound of bacon, and a couple pounds of turkey."

"Just give me a few minutes and I'll get Earl to round it up. Would you like your usual, as well?"

"Better make it two," Kyle said, motioning towards Katie.

Pearl looked over at Katie and winked. "Sure thing, dear."

"Hi," Katie said with a smile and a wave. Something about being around Pearl just made her feel at home.

"I almost forgot. Miss Price was looking for a place to use the internet," Kyle said.

Pearl raised her eyebrows. "It's not a request we get every day, but I think we can do something about that. Why don't we let Mr. Kyle rummage around out here and you can follow me to the back."

"Sounds like a plan," Katie said. She followed Pearl down the aisles and through the back door. She was still skeptical about internet access out here, but any doubt she had faded just a few steps into the backroom.

"Earl!" Pearl yelled. "If you'd ever pull your eyes away from those gosh-darn gizmos you'd know we have customers." Pearl turned back to Katie. "Sorry dear, believe it or not but he's obsessed with all this technology stuff."

Katie couldn't believe her eyes. Sitting in an old brown recliner in front of two huge television screens was another familiar face: Earl.

"You know they got an entire station about whales?"

"Earl!" Pearl yelled again from the doorway. "Miss Price here would like to use the internet."

At the mention of Katie's name, Earl snapped to attention. "Oh, Miss Price is back. Well, why didn't you tell me we had customers?"

Pearl just shook her head and Katie laughed. "You just tell Earl what you need and I'm sure we've got it. He's got all these satellite contraptions hooked up now." Pearl shut the door and walked back into the store, leaving Katie with Earl.

He walked over with a grin. "You seen them dogs, ain'tcha?"

"I have," Katie said.

"And?" he asked.

"They are amazing."

"I told you. Yep, I told you. I knew you'd like 'em."

"I do. And I'm very grateful. Pearl mentioned you might have a place I could get internet access?"

"Ah, yes, right this way."

* * *

Kyle sat down at the countertop in the back of the store while Pearl whipped up one of her delicious milkshakes.

"So you've got that beautiful young lady stayin' over at your place, I hear," Pearl said as she worked.

"You hear?"

"Small town," Pearl said with a grin.

"She's staying in the cottage. You know, with Mrs. Davis being gone and all…"

Pearl winked at Kyle. "Oh, I know. I tried to convince her not to go snoopin' around over there. How's Doc doin' these days?

"He's been keeping busy. Between Mrs. Perry having her baby, Mr. Willis' cows, and a few other house calls, I honestly haven't seen him much lately."

"Well, I'm glad to hear he's doing well. And how about you and your new writer *friend*? How are you two doing?"

Kyle fought back a smile. He should have known Pearl would have something to say about this. "It's nothing like that. She's just looking to use the dogs in one of her stories."

"Whatever you say, hon. Just remember that girls like that don't come around here very often."

Kyle swiveled around in his chair as the back door opened and Katie walked through. Earl followed, talking all the way.

"…four common whales in California? The gray whale, the humpback whale, the blue whale, and the fin whale. The blue whale can be over one hundred tons!"

"Earl! How many times do I gotta tell you the customers don't want to hear that nonsense?"

Earl looked up at Pearl with a straight face. "Everyone likes whales." Then he turned back around and walked right out the door still talking. "I mean, there is a whole television station on whales…"

"I'm sorry about that, dear," Pearl said as Katie walked up to the counter. "Did you get everything you needed?"

"Oh, the internet. Yes, thank you," Katie said.

Pearl picked up two full glasses and set them on the counter. "Peanut butter, chocolate ice cream, and a little bit of banana. You two enjoy. I'm going to try again to get Earl to cut those televisions off and pack up your order."

Once Pearl was out of earshot, Katie sat down on the stool next to Kyle. "I didn't peg you for a milkshake guy."

"Every Friday," Kyle said, pulling his glass towards him.

"Well, how do you know I'm a milkshake girl?" Katie asked, raising her eyebrows slightly.

Katie had this way about her when she asked questions. It was genuine curiosity—like she truly wanted to know the answer. Even now, he could tell she wasn't being coy. *She would probably wait here all day for me to answer even the simplest of questions.* He liked how active her mind was, how everything seemed to demand her attention, but he wished sometimes that she would just…relax. Katie tilted her head slightly and tucked a strand of hair behind her ear. *And then there's that look.*

Kyle reached for the glass in front of Katie. "Well, if you don't want it I can always go for two."

Katie slapped the back of his hand and pulled the glass towards her with both hands, biting down on the straw as she took a sip and smiled. "It just so happens that I do like milkshakes. But why chocolate and peanut butter?"

Kyle took another sip through his straw. "Because nothing goes better with chocolate than peanut butter."

"Like Colossus and Olympia?"

Kyle laughed. "What do you mean?"

"Well, Colossus is like chocolate and Olympia is like peanut butter."

"I never really thought of it that way, but yes, like Colossus and Olympia."

"How do you know which dogs to pair together, though?"

"Well…there's actually several theories on sled dog pairing. Some mushers want dogs of equal disposition or temperament. Some are more concerned with size or speed. For example, a shorter dog running next to a taller dog may create an uneven gait."

"What do *you* look for?"

Kyle hesitated for a moment. "I look for dogs who want to be together. You can analyze size, strength, speed, aggression, and so on until you're blue in the face. But ultimately every dog has a best friend, and those are the dogs I try to pair together."

"I like that."

"Like what?"

"The idea that dogs can be best friends."

He looked at the girl in front of him. Her jeans and boots were starting to get worn from all the work around the barn. Just under her right eye was a smudge of dirt, and a small piece of hay hung in her dark brown pony tail. Kyle had kept his distance from Katie since her arrival, giving her long lists of chore after chore to complete. It was just easier that way. She'd eventually finish her story and that'd be it. But did he really want that to be it?

"What?" Katie said. She ran her hand over the top of her head and brushed down the back of her neck. "Do I have something on me?"

She'll be gone in another day or so, he thought.

"We better get goin'," he said, finishing off his milkshake. "I'll grab the stuff from Pearl and meet you out front."

"Kyle," Katie said, as he started to walk away. "Thank you."

With his back to her, Kyle looked over his shoulder. He started to say something, but instead just touched his hand to the bill of his cap. Before he made it to the backdoor, he heard a familiar voice from the next room yell, "Kyle Merriman Walker!"

He turned back to Katie long enough for her to mouth, "Merriman?" then darted through the back door with Katie following.

Pearl wasn't in the backroom. In fact she wasn't in the store at all. She was moving through a crowd of chickens with a broom in her hand, swatting at a quick-moving black figure.

Kyle stepped outside and put his fingers to his lips, letting out a quick and piercing whistle. King ran to his side, several chicken feathers caught in his coat.

Not far behind was Pearl, who—surprisingly enough— was still moving at a good pace.

"When I get my hands on that dog...!"

Kyle didn't know whether to laugh or run. Earl made that decision for him. "You best be gettin' that dog out of here

119

now," he said, handing Kyle several bags of goods and Katie another. "Go on now. I'll see what I can do to fix this up." Kyle looked at Katie, who was already on the move around the side of the house with King a few steps behind. "Thanks, Earl."

A few minutes later, they were crossing the road and stepping back through the fence to Doc's property.

Kyle looked down at King. "I hope you had fun back there, because that's probably the last time you'll be going back for a while." King tilted his head, almost as if he was confused.

"He was just making some new friends," Katie joked. Holding the bag in one arm, she reached down towards King and scratched the top of his head. "Right, boy?"

Kyle stood and watched as King pressed his ears flat against his neck in anticipation of Katie's hand. She ran her fingers over the dog's head and down to the soft fur of his neck and back, with no idea of the significance of the moment – no idea that she was the first person to touch King besides Kyle or Doc.

21

ONCE THEY REACHED THE SLED, Kyle strapped down the three bags of groceries with a piece of rope. The basket was a little crammed, but Katie didn't mind. Kyle went through the same series of commands as before and the dogs moved as smoothly as a set of cogs in a machine.

The wind was cool against Katie's face as they rushed over the land. The dogs had been restless when she and Kyle got back, and now they used that energy to move at an even greater speed on their way home.

Katie looked back up at Kyle. His eyes were squinted against the setting sun and the rushing wind. His calloused hands wrapped around a steel rod covered in black tape. *I'm glad I'm here*, she thought.

"Gee," Kyle called out. The dogs made a slight left turn around a row of slender pines and the brick-red barn came into view. On the back hung a faded yellow star with lines of rust seeping down the red wood. *Star rust*, Katie thought, mentally making a note to write that down later.

When they pulled into the barn Kyle walked over to help Katie out of the sled, but she hopped out on her own. Instead he walked towards the front of the dogs and began to unclip them one at a time, checking their paws before putting them back in their pens.

"I can take the groceries in while you do that," Katie said.

Kyle looked up at Katie. "I can do it, just gotta finish with the dogs first."

"First you don't want me to do anything but chores, now I can't even help?" Katie picked up the two bags of groceries, one in each arm and turned towards the house. "You need to make up your mind."

Kyle watched her as she walked until Story jumped up and licked his face. He pushed her off playfully and laughed. "Do I lick you when you're in the middle of something?" When he looked back up all he saw was the front door swinging shut behind her.

* * *

Kyle took his boots off and set them by the front door. Through the screen he could hear the simmer of the stove.

"Dinner will be ready in a minute," Doc said as Kyle walked in.

Doc looked back at him as Kyle looked around the dining room and towards the wash room. "She's not here."

"Who?" Kyle said.

Doc shook his head at the sauté pan in front of him full of chili. "Who? We get so many cute, young brunettes around here that you have trouble remembering them."

"Okay, fine. Where is Miss Price?"

Doc lifted the pan with a gloved hand and used a spatula to push the steaming chili into two bowls.

"First off, stop calling the girl 'Miss Price.' I call her that because I'm old and it's respectful. Second off, she asked if she could take her dinner back to the cottage. Said she had some stuff to do, and I obliged."

Kyle didn't respond. He just sat down at the table as Doc placed a bowl of chili in front of him.

"Do me a favor, would you?" Doc said seriously. "Take both hands and grab your ears firmly."

Kyle hesitated, sensing something was coming, but he moved his hands over his ears.

"Now pull. You might just be able to remove your head from your ass. I hardly know the girl and I can tell you she's once in a lifetime." Doc picked up his bowl of chili and walked out to the porch, leaving Kyle to eat in silence.

22

THE NEXT MORNING, it was still dark when Katie opened her eyes. She closed the notebook that laid underneath her arm and set it on the nightstand. The curtains were drawn, but a faint glow of moonlight lingered around them. From across the room Katie heard the sound of her phone ring again.

She pulled the blanket over her head and let it go to voice mail.

The bedroom window was pulled open a few inches and a cool breeze fluttered through the room. The soft down comforter felt so good against her chilled skin, and the night air carried a certain peacefulness with it.

Until the phone rang again.

And again.

And again.

Finally, Katie groaned, pushed the comforter off her, and got out of bed. Across the room, the phone still vibrated on the chest of drawers.

It was her agent.

She glanced at the time before she answered.

5:17 a.m.

"There better be a good reason why you're waking me up for the second day in a row," Katie said as she smushed the phone against her face.

There was silence, then a deep breath.

"Absolutely amazing," Sam said.

"What is absolutely amazing?" Katie asked, still half asleep.

"This is going to be another bestseller."

"But I've hardly written a thing about the dogs yet, I finally just got to spend time with them yester—"

Sam interrupted her before she could finish. "The dogs? Forget about the dogs, this story is about the guy."

Katie was confused. "Doc? I hardly wrote about him, either."

"Oh, dear."

"What?"

"You've actually fallen for him."

"Fallen for who?"

"This just keeps getting better."

Katie heard her agent flipping through pages in the background.

"Page nineteen, 'His body was motionless as his hand rested upon the dog's chest. He wasn't doing a thing that I could see. Yet I knew that he was speaking the silent language of souls. And whatever souls are made of, in that moment his seemed to be made of more.' That's who."

"Wait, Kyle? You think I've fallen for Kyle? He's the whole reason I've hardly even seen the dogs! He's quiet and moody and completely impossible to read. Not to mention bossy. I spent almost my entire first week here doing his stupid chores. Then out of nowhere he's nice to me for a couple of days. I mean, he must wake up at like four a.m. every day to write those stupid notes. Which makes no sense to me. And sure, it's been like two days since I got one, but that's only because of what happened with Belle. Besides, what could he possibly be doing that early?

Katie hadn't realized she was rambling.

Sam laughed. "I rest my case. No woman gets that irritated by a guy unless she wants him."

"Seriously. I have no idea what you're talking about." Katie heard a resigned sigh on the other end of the line.

"Okay, fine. Play that way. The good news is, this piece you sent me last night got you an extension. It still needs a bit of work with your editor, but the story is fantastic. The bad news is, I turned that extension down for a bonus to go to print before Christmas. So, whatever you're doing, keep doing it. And send me the finished draft within the month. Oh, and one more question. Is he a good kisser?"

Katie hung up the phone and went back to bed.

The only problem was, now she couldn't sleep. Her eyes moved to the curtain dancing with the wind. She wrapped herself up tightly in the comforter, hugging one of the large pillows. As she closed her eyes, her mind raced. She thought about the story...about her time spent here over the last week. Then, she thought about the words she'd just said to Sam.

What could he possibly be doing at five a.m.? Before she knew it, Katie was up, dressed, and on her way out the door to find out.

23

WHEN KYLE WOKE it was still dark out. In fact, it would be dark out for a couple more hours. He pressed the Indiglo button on his Timex and the screen lit up with a bluish-green hue. Doc had given him this watch a few years back, and it was one of the few pieces of technology that he enjoyed. It had a built-in compass, a stop watch that was perfect for training with the dogs, and a world clock that displayed something like sixty-two cities. Of those sixty-two cities, San Diego seemed to come up more and more in his mind.

5:24 a.m.

Kyle pulled on his jeans and slipped on his boots. Standing in front of a two-drawer table next to his nightstand, he reached for a shirt, but the drawer was empty. He had forgotten to bring up the load of wash he'd done last night and knew it was sitting on top of the dryer in Doc's house, along with his hat.

He leaned over to the barn lamp sitting on his nightstand, pulled the glass globe off, and blew out the flame. The area around his bed dimmed and he placed the globe back down on the four brass prongs at the top of the lamp.

By the time he got to the bottom of the ladder, King was there waiting. Many of the other dogs were up and moving, but didn't pay him much attention. They had come to know his habits—he'd be back in an hour or so.

* * *

When Katie arrived at the barn, it was only a few minutes 'till six.

The barn door was ajar, with a small gap about three feet wide—plenty of space for her to step through.

She assumed the dogs were asleep before she stepped inside, but as she looked around she saw nothing but perked ears and pairs of yellow eyes following each step. The barn would have been pitch black except for the starlight that poured through the skylights.

Katie made her way across the barn until she stopped in front of Belle's pen. Curled up next to Belle were her four puppies. Three were curled up near her tummy, their arms, legs, and ears a tangled mess of cuteness, while the fourth had buried itself into the silky soft fur around Belle's neck. Belle lifted her head to acknowledge her and Katie smiled.

"Go back to sleep. You still need your rest," Katie whispered.

Belle obliged and laid her head back down atop a small fluff of hay.

A board creaked above Katie.

Was Kyle awake already? Was he in here with the dogs somewhere?

She had never thought to ask where Kyle stayed each night. Besides the bathroom and kitchen, she hadn't set foot any further into Doc's house—she'd just assumed both men had bedrooms in the trailer.

In the silence she heard the whispers of the night air rush past the barn door. Several purple petals from the tree just outside the barn swept past her. She watched as it dipped and fluttered upon the breeze until it landed softly on the rung of an old ladder. She kept walking until she reached the ladder, tucked away in the corner of an empty pen. It extended up towards a loft, a part of the barn that she had never even noticed in the daylight. Kyle had been very specific about her chores in the barn—not once had he mentioned anything about the loft.

She reached her hand out to a splintered rung about four feet off the ground. She must have walked past this ladder a hundred times in the past week, but never thought twice about it.

A cloud eased through the sky and the shadow of the moonlight on the wall darkened, but Katie didn't hear any sounds except the rustle of the dogs as they turned to watch her.

She placed another hand on the rung above and stepped onto the ladder. The rough wood felt surprisingly soft as her fingers pressed into each board. She couldn't say why she felt compelled to go up there, but she did.

Katie reached the top of the ladder and grabbed the railing on either side, pulling herself into the loft. When she looked to her right she was pretty sure she had her answer about where Kyle slept.

Set on a square nightstand built from several fruit pallets was an old-fashioned kerosene lamp. It was in the shape of a teardrop, with a cylindrical chamber on the bottom that was half full, but no flame was lit. On one side of the nightstand was a small table, on the other side a bed. There was no box spring, just a built-up timber stand about six inches off the ground and a mattress. A blanket was folded neatly at the end of the mattress and two pillows were stacked next to the barn wall that served as a headboard.

This was Kyle's room.

Katie knew she shouldn't be here. She knew Kyle wouldn't want her here. She should turn around and slowly ease herself back down the ladder, quietly stepping from one end of the barn to the other, out through the half-open barn door and back to the cottage. Instead, she started moving towards the lamp, towards the table, and towards a dark rectangular object that drew her attention.

She sat down on the edge of the bed and reached towards the small nob on the base of the lamp. It was the size of a penny, with rough edges like a cog wheel. She turned it clockwise slightly and the cotton wick extended, but no flame ignited.

Why can't there just be a light switch or something in here?

Sitting next to the lantern was a brown book. It was old, but it was canvas, not leather. She couldn't make out any title on the binding. She shifted her weight on the bed as she lifted the book off the table and a board creaked below her.

Katie moved her hands across the cover and binding, feeling the granular canvas cover and depressions that had been created by folding the cover back on itself over time. Her fingers moved slowly, as if she were searching for a trap door or secret chamber that would unlock another world.

She opened the book hesitantly, bending the cover back and angling the pages towards the light that crept in through a crack in the roof.

As she started to read, she heard the barn door creak open.

Shit. Kyle is back.

She slammed the book shut and shoved it into the drawer without thinking, almost knocking the lamp over as she quickly stood. The boards creaked again as she moved across the loft and towards the ladder. Too late, she realized her error.

Was the book inside the drawer, or on the table when I found it? He's going to kill me.

Katie took the steps two at a time as she nearly slid down the ladder and out of the loft. But when she reached the barn floor, she was alone. The barn door wasn't open any more than when she'd first arrived, and neither Kyle nor Doc were anywhere in sight. The dogs weren't stirring, but they were still alert, eyes fixed on her movement.

She brushed some timber debris off her hands and bent over halfway to sweep off her jeans. That's when she saw him.

Standing just inside the door where his black fur blended in with the morning shadows, was King.

He knew. She could see it in his eyes. But maybe he didn't care, because once he saw her he came trotting up to her. He opened his mouth and his tongue fell out to the side, panting as he rubbed his shoulder against her leg like a cat.

Katie held her finger up to her lips. "This will be our little secret."

She turned sideways and slipped back through the barn door the same way she had come in. The rising sun had just peaked the horizon. At the same time that she looked to the east, Kyle came jogging around the corner. Shirtless.

Sweat dripped down his chest and arms. His shoulders were wider than she had realized, accentuated by the v-shaped taper of his torso. His stomach was taut and her eyes followed it down to the line of his jeans, hanging just below his waist.

It occurred to Katie suddenly that maybe Sam wasn't so far off base after all. Because...wow.

He wasn't wearing a hat, either. It was the first time she'd seen him without one. His hair was dark brown, almost black. Short on the sides, and just enough to run her fingers through on the top. Katie moved to take a step towards him—except it wasn't a step at all, because her foot caught on a small rock embedded in a patch of clay and she tripped. She tried to break the fall with her arms, but she had been too distracted to recover quickly enough. As she hit the ground she let out a soft whimper, her shoulder driving hard into the dirt.

Kyle paused and looked down at her, stopping several feet away.

"There's a storm coming in," he said, walking past her and towards Doc's house.

"Don't worry, I'm fine," Katie remarked sarcastically as she stood up, brushing herself off for the second time that morning.

Or maybe Sam doesn't know what the hell she's talking about.

24

IT TOOK THEM SEVERAL HOURS to clean and secure the barn. Kyle was very specific about how he wanted everything—hay bales were to be stacked in a certain order, the rigging needed to be taken off the wall and banded together on the ground, water bowls had to be put away, and so on.

It was almost noon when Kyle stood at the entrance of the barn, his left hand pressed high against the timber frame as he looked out at the dark skies. Meanwhile, Katie silently counted the dogs as she walked past each pen.

"Thirty-one," she said, barely audible. "One is missing."

She looked over at Kyle standing just below the timber lintel. King wasn't standing next to him.

"King is missing," she said as she jogged up next to Kyle.

He looked at her solemnly, almost searching.

"Come with me," he said. "I want to show you something."

Did he not hear me? King is missing.

Before she could say anything Kyle started off, walking briskly in the direction of the storm. He looked up to the sky several times and then broke into a light jog. His version of a light jog had Katie gasping for air when they stopped almost ten minutes later, next to an enormous oak tree.

Katie recognized this place. Doc had called it Old Man's Crossing on her first day here. She could remember seeing the dogs and Kyle for the first time. Looking at him now, he seemed so different. He had been so distant when they first met. Not just physically, but even when she'd been with him it was like his mind was always somewhere else. Now, he was taking her to secret places. Now, he was including her.

He turned to her, interrupting her thoughts. "Do not make a sound."

Kyle crept slowly behind the large oak that stood several paces in front of them. Then, he crouched down and motioned for her to do the same.

He looked into the distance. The storm was still moving in, but now it looked like it had slowed down, like a train pulling into the station. It was so dark that it was hard to tell just how hard the rain was coming down in the distance. Huge vertical sheets of it created an expanse that almost looked like a giant mirror in the sky.

Kyle remained quiet, just stared across the small valley created by two hills a few hundred feet apart.

Katie didn't understand what they were doing. Was this another one of his games? She looked in the same direction he was, but saw nothing.

A few minutes passed and still Kyle sat there, crouched like a catcher waiting for the pitch.

Finally Katie whispered, "What are we looking for?"

Apparently expecting the question, Kyle simply pointed across the field to the farthest hill. "Be patient. Just watch."

Something in the distance slowly moved along the subtle ridgeline of the hill farthest from them.

Katie's muscles tensed as she watched a black figure climb the slope.

King.

He stood silent, facing the storm, and lifted his nose to the wind.

Without warning, white lightning ripped through the rain and echoed over the land. King turned towards the downslope with blurring speed, as if nature had fired the starting gun. He crossed the field in a matter of seconds as he raced towards them.

The dark sky let out a loud rumble and another flash of yellow blazed from the clouds.

Kyle raised his hand to his forehead as if to shield his eyes as King continued across the vast landscape. The sky opened up around them and rain poured down.

Katie brushed the cold water from her arms, barely registering the fact that she was getting wet. She couldn't take her eyes off King. Every movement he made seemed to have a specific purpose. It was similar to being in the sled, but this time he ran free.

He turned slightly to the left just before he approached a small divot, and then back right to avoid a thick patch of grass. He moved at a furious pace, unlike anything Katie had ever seen before.

As he passed, Kyle stood and walked to the edge of the tree line, his eyes still following King.

Katie followed, both of them just watching.

Katie didn't understand why the mere image of a dog running seemed to overwhelm her. She had seen lots of dogs run. But there was something different about this; something deeper. As a writer she hated clichés, but this time it was true.

"Is he running from the rain?" Katie asked.

"Not from it," Kyle said as he lunged out from under the cover of the foliage and into the rain. "Before it." His steps were light as he moved. One step slightly balanced towards the right and then cut back towards the middle.

Katie couldn't help but wonder, *Does Kyle run like King or does King run like Kyle?*

Not sure what else to do, she followed Kyle out into the rain. Head down, she ran after him, focused on the feel of cold raindrops on the back of her neck, her thin cotton shirt plastered to her skin

"Let's go!" she heard Kyle shout.

She looked up when she heard Kyle's voice. He was soaking wet, his face turned towards her with a huge smile across it as he continued running. Then Katie realized she was smiling too. She picked up speed as she approached Kyle and yelled as she passed, "I'm winning!"

"Oh no you're not!" Kyle shouted after her as he took off again.

They both ran at full speed, until the rain began to turn the ground in front of them into a slippery slope of mud and grass. Katie slowed down to catch herself in time to watch Kyle slip and go down as he tried to run and shout something at the same time.

Katie stopped next to him, gasping for breath as she mocked him. "There's a storm coming."

Before she could move away, he grabbed her arm and pulled her down with him.

She laughed as she fell on top of him, one hand landing on his chest, the other palm first into the wet ground. Katie lifted her head. She was just inches from Kyle. They paused for a brief moment, looking at one another before Katie swiped a muddy finger below his cheek.

Kyle's eyes darkened and his expression went serious. Katie stopped moving. "I have a question for you," Kyle said.

"Okay. What is it?" she said, trying to catch her breath, suddenly a little nervous.

He remained serious, letting the moment hang between them. "Are you ticklish?"

Katie couldn't move fast enough. Kyle's hands wrapped around her waist as he tickled her sides, just below her ribs.

"Kyle Merriman Walker!" she shouted. She was laughing so hard it hurt as he rolled her off him and onto her back. His knees straddled her waist and his hands planted on the ground next to her face. He leaned closer to her and wiped away several strands of wet hair. She reached for his waist and hooked her thumbs inside the top edge of his jeans, and pulled him closer. It was still raining hard, but all Katie could feel was the unrelenting beat of his heart.

That's when Katie heard a sound she would never forget.

* * *

When Katie thought of howling, she pictured a wolf standing on a silver mountain, head arched towards a full moon. The incessant hoot of a great horned owl, the rushing waters of the river's deep, and the indescribable cadence of a deer's hooves against the ground—all silenced by his presence. She imagined the wolf strong and fearless as he howled, the call careening off the mountain peaks and traveling through the valley. All of nature gone still around him.

But the sound Katie heard now was far from that.

It was a few hours after daybreak, but most everything around her was covered in the storm's shadow, save the buzzing lamp light hanging next to the barn door.

The first howl was piercing. It was not calm or smooth, it was sharp and desperate. Startling. There was no other way to describe it. She didn't just hear it, she felt it.

Katie turned her eyes towards the sound, barely able to make out the dark figure eclipsed by the falling rain. Kyle stood up and stared at the dark figure in the distance. She shielded the rain and wind from her eyes as she sat up, and looked again. It was King.

He lifted his muzzle towards the sky and let out another piercing shriek that caused her entire being to shake.

Something was wrong. Very wrong.

25

KATIE HAD NEVER UNDERSTOOD why people run. And yet without fail each morning in California, hundreds of runners plod over the beach or along city streets without purpose, sweat dripping off their brow or soaking into their clothes. And for what? So they could eat a few extra French fries with their burger for lunch? Or throw back several drinks guilt-free at the bar after work?

But now, she put one foot down in front of the other. Heel, toe. Heel, toe. Heel, toe. Suddenly, she began to understand the impetus to run—particularly when there was something to run towards.

She was several hundred feet behind Kyle when he reached King, but they didn't pause to wait for her. Katie stopped to catch her breath at the spot where they had been standing, and looked down towards the barn.

King was nowhere in sight, and Kyle was sliding the barn doors wide open. Everything had seemed so quiet after the piercing howl, but suddenly a cacophony of barks, yips, and howls drowned out her thoughts.

Katie took several more steps, still catching her breath. And then she saw it—smoke rising from a charred hole at one end of the barn.

The barn was on fire.

The smoke was subtle at first, like a slow whisper on the ground. The orange flame built towards the far end of the barn. The red paint started to char black and flake off into the wind, now feeding the flames with more and more oxygen.

Kyle turned, his gaze fixed on Katie's for a moment, as if he knew that she'd been standing there watching the scene unfold. Then he disappeared into the barn after King.

An unexpected shriek escaped Katie's mouth. "No!"

Katie ran towards him, almost tripping over Belle as the dog trotted out of the barn, shaking the smoke off her body. Behind Belle, Kyle followed with four black balls of fur wrapped in his arms. The puppies.

Not breaking stride, he pushed the puppies into Katie's arms and said, "Get all the dogs in the house. Now." And again he disappeared back into the smoke-filled barn. The slow-moving darkness engulfed him like a thick fog.

Katie watched as he rushed from pen to pen, flipping the latch up so the gates would swing freely. King followed behind him, flicking gates open with his nose and herding the dogs towards Katie with a ferocious growl and determined eyes.

This went on for several minutes. Katie watched from a distance as some of the younger dogs cowered from the heat, unsure what to do as Kyle and King sprinted from pen to pen. Kyle had to double back several times and grab a dog by the scruff, dragging them out as they whined.

It was easier to get the dogs into the house than Katie had expected. Once they stopped coming out she began to count, as she had done earlier.

One, two, four, seven, twelve, thirteen, fifteen, sixteen, twenty, twenty-two, thirty-one.

She looked around and counted again. And again it was thirty-one.

She shut the door to the house and ran down the porch steps towards the barn. About twenty feet away, she started to feel the heat. The rain still fell hard against the scorched barn, but the fire was building from within.

Where is Kyle? Where is King?

Katie cupped her hands together and shouted his name, but the elements were too overwhelming to carry her voice more than a few feet.

Where was he?

She knew what she was about to do was a bad idea, but her feet were already moving forward, her hand in front of her pushing past the smoke.

The air was hot as she entered the barn, and the smoke was dark and thick, trapped within, and getting worse. The sound of the fire was deafening, coming at her from every direction. The flames cracked like a thousand tiny whips, and the timber beams groaned as they tried to resist the bright orange heat.

Katie was coughing hard by the time she reached the ladder, her eyes stinging from the rise of black smoke all around her. There was no hesitation this time as she scurried up, but when she reached the top Kyle wasn't there. The flames were starting to climb the walls around her, and she knew she had made a mistake.

"Katie!" she heard Kyle shout from below. "Katie!"

It was too late.

The fire devoured the kerosene from the oil lamp in a flash of scorching flame. The lamp exploded in front of Katie before she could react, sending a sudden burst of noise, light, and heat throughout the barn. The eruption knocked Katie back against the loft railing, which broke instantly.

The main vertical member holding up the loft fought to stand tall, but the onslaught of kinetic energy was too much to overcome.

The loft collapsed.

And there was nothing but darkness.

26

KYLE'S FIRST BREATH was little more than a cough, as he sucked in air full of carbon and hydrocarbon burned off from the barn timbers. He shook his head and tried to clear the air in front of him by waving his hand back and forth several times. The smoke burned his eyes as he swatted at it, but he was able to take short breaths. Breathing wasn't his only problem, though.

As Kyle pushed his palms into the hard ground, a sharp pain shot up both his legs. He couldn't sit up all the way. Panic rose in his chest. Braced on his elbows, he could see one of the large timbers that once supported the loft laying across his thighs.

He wiggled his toes. He wasn't paralyzed, at least he didn't think so, but that wasn't his main concern. He didn't see Katie.

He looked around.

Behind him and to his right, orange and red flames consumed the barn. To his left, the dog pens lay empty and still untouched. And directly in front of him, the entrance was still clear. He had no idea how much longer he had until the fire ate its way to him, but it was likely to be counted in minutes or seconds.

A dark object nearly ran into him. A soot-covered tongue lapped at his face. "King!" Kyle yelled urgently, though the dog was still standing over him. "Where's Katie?" King just stood there panting heavily.

Kyle repeated the word, "Katie." But this time he also formed the number two with his right hand and pointed at his eyes.

Show me Katie.

Kyle followed King's line of sight as King lifted his head slightly and looked directly at the practice sled. Less than two feet to the left of Kyle, between himself and the dog pens, sat the sled. The two wheels farthest from him lay on the ground in pieces. The impact of Katie landing on the sled had easily broken the wheels, which weren't meant to carry much weight.

Katie's right arm lay palm up, hanging over the side panel. Kyle could see the top of her left knee pointing at him. The rest of her body was hidden from view.

"Katie!" Kyle shouted.

No response.

"Katie!"

Still nothing.

When Kyle looked back down at his legs, he realized it wasn't just one beam sitting on top of him, it was several. And on top of them, broken floorboards and some other scraps. He was pinned. All but buried.

His heart began to race as reality set in. A charred piece of wood fell and when he looked up he saw the dark sky in place of a piece of the roof. The fire was definitely a concern, but as he looked around at the orange flames he knew the structure would collapse long before he would be burned. Even worse, the smoke was building into a thick gray cloud. He wouldn't have to worry about being buried alive, because soon he wouldn't be able to breathe.

Kyle closed his eyes and covered his mouth with the sleeve of his shirt, trying to suck in a few short breaths of clean air. It didn't work—he was coughing now as much as he was breathing. He tried to pull his legs out one more time, but there was no hope. Nothing even budged.

"Agghhhhh!" he screamed, the panic setting in.

King licked at his face again and whimpered. Kyle reached over, instinctively touching the dog.

Calm.

He breathed in slowly and began to search for something he could possibly use as a lever. The beams were too heavy to lift completely off his legs, but he might be able to raise them high enough to slide out.

Against one of the rails was the rake he used to clean out the pens, but it would snap in an instant under that much pressure. On the tool bench he could see a hammer, which might be strong enough but definitely not long enough to use as a lever. He kept scanning the barn. There had to be something he could use.

Sure enough, there was.

Towards the entrance of the barn was a pile of fresh two by fours left over from building the top rail of the new dog pens. Unfortunately, there were two problems—they were more than twenty feet from him, and he had never taught King a word that was remotely close to two by four or timber. Still, he had to try.

145

King was lying next to Kyle, panting from the heat.

"King," Kyle said slowly, making sure he had eye contact with him.

King was already staring straight at Kyle, but at the sound of his words he drew in his tongue and closed his mouth, waiting for the next command.

Kyle held up his hand and formed the number five, then closed it into a fist grabbing at the air. Then he pointed directly at the stack of lumber and again made the hand gesture for retrieve.

Retrieve the timber.

King slowly turned, knowing there had been a command given, but unsure of exactly what it was. He trotted towards the entrance of the barn directly next to the two by fours, turned, and sat down.

This time, Kyle pointed with his right hand towards the wood and used his left hand to make the symbol for retrieve.

King moved to his right and scented the ground in front of the two by fours, then began to lift his nose to them as well.

That's it, boy.

He licked the base of one near a small knot in the pine, and then he opened his mouth and bit down on the two by four gingerly. As King began to pull the piece of wood towards him, a pile of burning shingles fell to the ground. King juked left, letting the pile fall beside him, then grabbed a board and began to drag it towards Kyle.

Kyle smiled in relief, until another chunk of the ceiling crashed to the floor about thirty feet away from him—right next to King, who dropped the two by four and darted out of the barn.

Kyle covered his face with this hands, feeling the ash and soot on his hot skin. *This isn't going to work.*

Part of him wanted to give up. His eyes were burning, his lungs were deprived of oxygen, and he was pinned to the ground. He looked over at Katie lying lifeless in the sled.

I can't give up.

Another piece of timber fell next to his shoulder, and Kyle jolted to the right. As he turned back, though, he realized it was King. With the two by four.

He pushed it alongside his right leg and slightly underneath one of the beams that pinned him. There was just enough room to turn the board on its side, which would make the lever much stronger and allow Kyle to push with more force.

Something didn't feel right, though. The timber was too light as Kyle pushed it in place. As soon as he lifted one end up against the fallen beam, it snapped. Then it dawned on Kyle—the heat had dried out the wood.

Kyle threw the board down and let his head fall back to the ground. As he looked up at Katie, he could see the fire behind her spreading quickly through the stalls. The hay scattered through the pens, only adding to the gray powdered smoke.

He looked back down at his legs and struggled furiously. At first he felt his legs move slightly, but then some of the boards gave way and caved in around the free space that he had just created, pinning him even more tightly.

Kyle groaned and tried again, fighting to pull his legs free until it felt like he might dislocate his knee. It was no use.

He looked over at Katie, still motionless on the sled. He thought about the first time he'd seen her—how impossible she'd been from the start. All those questions. There was something about her, though. He'd done everything he could to hide it, knowing that she was leaving—that a girl like her would never have any real interest in someone like him.

As Kyle laid there ready to give up, he saw something in his periphery. At first he'd missed it, but as his thoughts caught up he jerked his head around until he was staring at an empty harness lying on the ground. His eyes followed the harness across the floor to the three others still banded neatly together. One must have fallen free during the fire.

A breeze of cool air swept through the barn as several drops of rain started to fall around him. There was still hope.

27

"FOCUS," KYLE SAID TO KING after he hooked the final latch on the harness.

It meant, *Look at me.* Ignore everything around you. Forget about the fire, the heat, the smoke. Forget about the night breeze only a trot away or the timbers that crashed to the floor. *Focus.*

Kyle gave King the hand symbol for harness, using his index finger to draw a circle in the air. It was a signal King had seen a thousand times, and he didn't hesitate to retrieve the harness. Most sled dogs weren't trained for simple tasks like this. They were trained to run. Trained to win. But Kyle trained them to do so much more. He trained them to survive.

King dropped the harness on the ground next to Kyle. It was a struggle to clasp the harness around King's back without sending a searing pain down Kyle's pinned legs. But after several seconds, Kyle heard the unforgettable click as the clasp locked into place. King had no collar on, so Kyle was only able to connect the tug line to the harness.

Then he pulled on King's harness until he was face to face with his old friend. "I need you to do something," Kyle said, talking to King as if he understood every single word.

"I need you to do something that will be hard. But I need you to do it."

King gazed intently at Kyle, not moving, not blinking. His eyes were so still Kyle could barely see them for all the dark fur.

Kyle gave the initial command to King. A command he had given thousands of times over the years.

"Line out."

King walked to the front of the sled until the tow line was full of tension. Then he looked back at Kyle and waited.

Kyle had been so busy trying to find a way to free his legs that he hadn't noticed how quickly the fire had spread. Three sides of the barn were burning orange and red. The closest vertical pole next to him was black with char and he could hear the wood crackle and pop all around him.

As King sat there, Kyle thought about the reality of what he was asking King to do. The wooden sled—really more a wagon than a sled—was primarily built of southern pine on a hollow steel frame. It normally sat on four metal spools that Kyle had fashioned into wheels. With no load, the entire assembly probably weighed seventy-five pounds.

During the occasional trip to the store, a small team of dogs might pull the sled plus another twenty-five pounds of dog food and miscellaneous supplies for the barn. Several of the larger wheel dogs alone had pulled lighter loads during training, but it was seldom. There was no sense in training a single dog to pull that much weight when an entire team of fourteen to fifteen dogs would pull no more than four hundred pounds total—or about thirty pounds each.

King was strong, but as Kyle stared back at him he began to think of how old he looked. His pure black coat was tinged with gray and white fur around his nose, mouth, and eyes. The sheen of his coat had dulled a bit. His eyes looked tired and aged. But Kyle also saw something else. Past the rising panic, beyond the smoke and flames. He saw his friend.

King pawed at him, as if to say, *Let's do this.*

A deafening crack broke through Kyle's thoughts as the corner pole supporting the other end of the loft collapsed. It fell away from Kyle, which at first he thought was a good thing—until the top end of the pole smashed right through the side of the barn.

King jumped and jerked as the pole landed, trying to throw the harness free.

A gust of cold night air mixed with near-horizontal rain came rushing in. For a moment the heat seemed to subside. Then suddenly the fire exploded across the roof, as if someone had turned a temperature knob all the way to high.

Kyle shielded his face as the flames licked at the ceiling.

Without any more hesitation, Kyle gave the simplest command he had for the dogs.

"Lead on," he said between coughs.

King snapped to attention and turned towards the open barn door. The cable attached to the harness tightened, as did the nylon straps wrapped around King's shoulders and stomach. His paws dug into the bare floor and the sled creaked, but it didn't budge.

King looked back at Kyle a little confused, but Kyle had no answers to offer. With the cart on four wheels, this may have been possible after breaking the initial friction. But with one wheel broken and an edge in the dirt, each move King made was like starting over.

"Lead on," Kyle said again, with more urgency.

Another booming crack echoed through the barn as the door farthest from them fell flat to the ground. The hinges were still intact, but the wood around them was burned straight through.

King backed up two steps and let some slack into the taut line. He gathered as much momentum as he could and lunged forward as Mother Nature continued to chew through the barn.

The back right of the sled, where the wheel had broken off, moved slightly, creating a small crack in the muddy ground a couple inches long.

King's front paws dug furiously, his back paws firm against the ground.

Kyle shouted, "Lead on!"

King recoiled, again letting some slack in the line, and then burst forward with a fierce growl. He barked and yipped loudly, using the full range of his vocal cords. The cart lurched forward again, but was only a foot farther than where it started. They were still twenty feet from the opening.

As King was about to let up Kyle screamed, "Lead on!"

King shook his head to the left towards Kyle, baring his teeth. He backed off the line yet again as he lowered all his weight onto his thick hind legs and jumped forward. The cable tightened and the cart barely moved, but King instantly repeated the motion again. And again. And again. He didn't stop for what seemed like hours to Kyle, as he literally dragged the cart inch by inch across the floor.

King's coat was matted against his body in ash and rain. The ground behind him was a battlefield of blood and grime, his right front paw bleeding from a piece of splintered wood. His breath was strained, each pull of the cart knocking all the wind from him. But as Kyle watched, King did not once let up.

He lunged forward biting at the air, defying the dead weight of the dragging cart. Daring it not to obey his efforts. He was the lead dog. This was his sled. And while Kyle would have refused the use of the term, this was his master.

And suddenly, King was out the door with Katie still in the back of the sled. A couple more feet and she would be clear. The cool air was upon him, the heat dissipating, but his master called out one last time.

"Lead on, King! Lead on!"

Kyle watched the straps tighten again around King, knowing his muscles were beat, if not broken. King was panting hard and yet somehow he summoned more strength than Kyle ever thought possible. He lunged forward and nearly broke into a run, dragging the cart almost five feet in one single motion.

Kyle gave King the command to stop as he looked out towards him.

Then, suddenly Kyle heard screaming.

Katie?

No, it was a male voice. He couldn't make out the words. His eyes burned so badly he could hardly open them. But he knew it must be Doc. As Doc reached the door, a huge section of the roof came tumbling down. The majority of the timbers missed Kyle, but pieces bounced off his stomach and arms as he shielded his eyes. The dust and smoke combined to make it nearly impossible to see.

As he turned his head back to the entrance, the last image he saw was that of King collapsing.

And there was darkness again.

28

KATIE ROLLED OVER on the couch, pulling her arm from underneath her, and tried to shake the sleep from it. She opened and closed her hand several times as she felt the needle-like sensation run down her forearm and shoulder.

When she opened her eyes, she didn't see the morning sun spilling in through the white curtains of the cottage. Instead, she saw Doc sitting across from her in a rocking chair with Belle and the pups on the floor by his side.

At just a few days old they were so tiny, curled up next to their mother for warmth. None of them had even opened their eyes yet. It wasn't until she heard Doc's voice that Katie began to remember.

"How are you feeling?" he asked.

She wanted to answer, to let him know she was fine even though her head was throbbing, her ribs ached, and her shoulder felt like it had been hit by a truck. She could only think of one thing, though.

"Where's Kyle? We have to help Kyle." Panicked, she nearly fell off the sofa as she tried to sit up.

She had startled Belle, who looked back at her with the eyes of a worried mother.

"Miss Price, please don't try to get up," Doc said as he tried to push her gently back down. "You're in no condition for that right now."

"But Kyle," she said again.

"Kyle will be fine. He's asleep in the other room."

"What about…the fire…and…the barn. And King. I couldn't find King."

"Everybody is fine," Doc said. "The fire is taken care of, the barn is fine, and the dogs are fine. But you, Miss, need to get some rest. You bumped your noggin pretty hard."

She couldn't remember. The only thing she could remember was the fire. The heat. The loud crackling noises as it spread throughout the barn. The thick plume of smoke that kept getting darker and darker as it rose upwards in the barn. One minute she was standing on the loft, the next she was waking up on the couch. There was no in between.

Doc pulled out a small flashlight as Katie lay back down, and moved it from eye to eye.

"You have a mild concussion. But you'll be fine with a little food and some rest."

Katie knew something was wrong, but her head still throbbed and felt so heavy, even lying on the pillow. She closed her eyes with Doc still kneeling by her side. As she let exhaustion drag her back to sleep, several images returned to her memory. The only one she could focus on was Doc kneeling beside her. But it wasn't her he was looking over. It was King.

When Katie woke for the second time, Doc was gone. She was in an empty room filled with the orange hue of a setting sun.

She pulled the blanket off and sat up on the couch. Her head was no longer throbbing, but the pain that shot up her left side caused her to wince. She tried to stretch her left arm, but realized she couldn't. It was in a sling, which she didn't recall putting on. Instinctively, she reached over with her right hand and ran it over the top of her left arm. Her shoulder hurt to touch, but the rest of the arm felt fine.

As she went to stand up she almost toppled over as the blood rushed back into her legs and feet.

How long have I been asleep?

She scanned the living room for a clock, but found nothing but the numbers on the microwave, the square green analog digits too blurry to make out.

As she reached the kitchen she heard the clang of something metal. The front door slowly eased open and Doc stepped inside.

His hands were covered in dirt and there was a ring of sweat around the collar of his shirt. There was no smile on his face, and Katie knew the words he had whispered to her earlier were a lie.

"Where is Kyle?" she asked frantically.

"Kyle is fine."

"That's not what I asked."

Doc motioned towards the back of the house. "He's still sleeping. You can go in if you'd like, but he still needs to rest.

His legs are bruised badly and he took a pretty good blow to the head, as well."

Katie still wasn't satisfied with the answer. She wanted to see for herself. But as she approached the bedroom door, she suddenly stopped.

Like a detective piecing together clues to a mystery, the gears in her head began to turn.

Why are Doc's hands dirty? If everything is okay, why doesn't he look like his usual self? What am I missing?

She turned around, and looked at Doc. But it was the object behind him that caught her eye. Just past the screen door, she saw a shovel leaning against the house. She could only mouth the name as she settled on the answer. *King.*

A single tear streamed down her cheek.

Doc still stood at the door, vainly wiping the dirt from his hands down the front of his jeans.

When their eyes met he could do nothing but nod, and the pain in Katie's shoulder felt like nothing compared to the pain in her heart as she fell to her knees.

She closed out the world as she brought both hands over her eyes and buried her face between her knees. Katie winced as pain shot through her shoulder and she quickly dropped her arm back into the sling, the physical pain only making things worse.

When she finally looked up, Doc was sitting next to her on the floor, his knees bent in front of him and his back against the wall.

"How?" she asked.

"As much as he didn't look it, he was an old dog. It was just too much stress on his heart."

"But I don't understand. I don't remember anything but the fire."

"Miss Price, I wish I had the answers, but I just don't know. I was on my way back from the Johnston's. Cal had cut his hand pretty deep with a circular saw. By the time I arrived, the rain had just about put out the fire, but there was still a giant stack of smoke that stretched nearly to the clouds. I got to the barn as fast as I could.

"I found you first. You were on top of the sled, lying on your back. Your left arm was bent underneath you," Doc continued as he pointed towards her sling. "You just about dislocated your shoulder."

"What about King?"

He closed his eyes, seemingly fighting tears.

"I carried you to the house and went back for Kyle. That's when I first saw King. He was lying on his side still tethered to the sled, not moving. I felt for a pulse, but as I placed my hand on his chest I realized he wasn't breathing. I tried to revive him, but it was no use. And I still didn't know where Kyle was...I had to leave King.

"Near the center of the barn I found Kyle. One of the main timber columns had snapped in several pieces over his legs. I had to get my truck to drag the timbers off him. Once his legs were free, it took me a while to get him inside. I had lost track of time at that point. I don't know if an hour passed or ten minutes. But after I knew you and Kyle were okay, I went back for King.

"I was just too late. Even if I had started with King, it wouldn't have mattered. I believe he passed long before I got there." Doc paused and rubbed the wrinkles on his forehead with both hands. "It didn't make sense at first. King wouldn't have left Kyle's side, unless..."

"Unless what?" Katie asked.

He paused. "Unless he was asked to."

"But why was he tied to the sled?" Katie said, realizing the answer almost immediately.

"Because it was the only way to save you."

"It's my fault," Katie said as she stood up. The realization shook her. "It's my fault. After we let all the dogs out, I couldn't find Kyle. I searched the main floor of the barn, but didn't see him. That's when I went up to the loft. I knew I had made a mistake the minute I was up there. I was scared; I wasn't thinking."

"I probably would have done the same thing," Doc said, trying to console her.

Katie looked at Doc, searching for the right words. Only six kept repeating in her head.

King is dead because of me.

29

DOC STOOD IN FRONT OF THE SINK after he had showered and dressed. He had scrubbed his hands until they hurt, but he still couldn't get all the dirt off them. The dirt that he used to bury King was stuck under his nails, and in the creases of his hands, like an unwanted memory.

He ran his hands under the warm water one last time, and splashed some over his face.

He looked back in the mirror and almost didn't recognize the man staring back at him. He pressed his hands into the deep wrinkles of his forehead. Was this the same man that fell in love with Hannah all those years ago?

It wasn't. He didn't want to admit it but it was true. Without her life had weighed heavier on him, and he wished more than anything she was still here.

Hannah would know what to do better than him, he thought. She always did. As he walked down the hall he could see Katie clutching a small pillow to her chest as she watched Kyle sleep. She sat with her knees curled up to her chest, running her hand over the fringe where some of the stitching had come undone.

Doc leaned against the doorway, the aged wood creaking softly under his weight. He looked over at Katie. "He'll be fine, Miss Price."

Katie clenched her jaw, flaring the small muscles just below her ears.

"I have some dinner on the stove. Why don't you come have a bite to eat?"

She looked down at her feet as they touched the floor and she sat forward. For a moment she just sat there, and Doc thought he may have to help her out of the room. But she managed to finally stand.

At that very moment, Kyle lifted his left hand. Katie's eyes flashed to his, but they were still closed.

"Doc," Katie called, even though he was still standing in the doorway.

"His hand. What is he doing?" Katie said, pointing towards the bed.

Kyle's eyes were still shut, but his hand was slightly raised above the bed. His fingers opened and then closed, almost as if he were slowly waving.

Doc looked back at Katie with eyes full of sorrow.

"He's just dreaming." Doc said.

He knew Katie could tell he was lying.

"Come. Let's get you something to eat."

Katie walked past Doc as he lightly touched her back, guiding her out of the room. He looked at Kyle once more, knowing full well what Kyle was really doing.

He was calling for King.

* * *

Katie sat down at the table, where Doc had already set two plates and some silverware. A black iron crock pot simmered on the stove. Doc went into the kitchen, lifted the clear glass top, and looked inside. "Perfect timing."

He looked over at Katie. "I hope you like chicken and dumplings." He grabbed two bowls and filled them to the brim, carefully walking them back to the table.

Doc didn't even wait for it to cool before he took a bite. Katie just sat there and watched as her food let off wave after wave of steam.

"You do like chicken and dumplings, right?" he asked.

She forced a smile. "I do. I was just thinking." Doc took another bite and followed it with a big gulp of water. "What's Kyle's story?" she asked.

"You mean with the dogs?"

"No, he told me about the origin of the dogs."

Doc raised an eyebrow.

"It just doesn't add up though. I mean, I get it, he loves those dogs and loves training, and that's why he stays. But..." Katie trailed off.

"But...?"

Katie paused for a moment, thinking about the best way to ask the question. "Every character has a plot, a reason for being. Kyle's plot, you could say, is training the dogs. But what's underneath all that? What's his motivation to see that plot through to the end?" She hated the analogy even as she said it.

Doc set the water down and looked down at his plate. She could sense the apprehension in his response. But to her surprise, he began to answer.

"It all started fourteen years ago. Kyle was just nine at the time. It was summer; I used to watch the boy for my sister – Kyle's mom – once school let out. The late-afternoon rain was falling furiously from the sky—that boy loved watching it rain. Didn't matter what time of the day, if it was raining, Kyle was on the porch watching.

"I can still remember the look in his eyes when I walked out of the house—it was as if he knew somehow. But, he didn't understand when I told him his parents wouldn't be coming to get him. I told him about their car going off the road, and it was like he didn't even hear me. Like nothing made sense." He paused, breathing in deeply.

"Day after day, he'd wait on the porch for them to pick him up, but they never came. He kept asking me when they'd be here. Eventually, I didn't know what to say anymore.

"One day when we were sitting on the porch, he turned to me and said something that no nine-year-old should ever think to say. He told me he had no hope left."

Katie wiped away several small tears from the corner of her eye.

"I grabbed him by the shoulder and pulled him to the bottom of the porch steps. I pointed towards the south, where the sky was dark and sheets of rain filled the space between the sky and the ground. Then I looked at him and said, 'There is hope all around us—in every breath, in every raindrop.'"

30

KATIE LAID DOWN on the couch after dinner. She was feeling better, but she didn't want to walk back to the cottage. Not without knowing Kyle was okay.

The space between each couch cushion made it difficult to get comfortable. She tried turning onto her side, and then her stomach, but no matter which way she laid Doc's last words replayed over and over in her mind.

There is hope all around us—in every breath, in every raindrop.

She had never heard anyone use those words, but her father.

When she finally woke again it was still dark outside. It had been over a day since the fire and, surprisingly, the pain in her arm was already subsiding. Or maybe that was just the painkillers that Doc had given her. Either way, as she took the sling off and stretched her arm, it felt better.

The house was silent as she sat up on the couch. She scanned the living room and kitchen, half expecting to find Doc making breakfast or just sitting there looking over her. He was nowhere to be found.

She wiped the sleep from her eyes and walked down the hall to Kyle's room, but when she opened the door, the bed was empty. He was gone, too.

Katie didn't know if this was good or bad. Her mind began to race. Was he okay and gone of his own volition, or had he gotten worse in the night? What if Doc had to rush him to the nearest hospital?

In the back of her mind, she heard Kyle's voice.

Calm.

Instead of rushing out of the house, she realized in the worst-case scenario she couldn't do anything. Kyle was sure to be fairly close—Doc wouldn't just let him wander off if he was in any real danger. Still, she wanted to find him.

She only made it to the top of the first step before the screen door closed behind her and she heard a welcome voice. "Well, good morning." Doc was seated casually in his rocking chair with a cup of coffee between both hands.

"Kyle is gone?" Katie asked.

"This is true," Doc nodded as he sipped his coffee.

"Is he okay?"

"I suspect not."

"Do you know where he is?"

"I do not."

"Dr. Anderson, I'm doing my best to remain calm, but your answers aren't exactly helping."

"I'm sorry," Doc said, looking down at the steam rising from the hot liquid. "I'm just not sure there's anything we can do right now. At least, nothing *I* can do."

"I'm a writer. You're a doctor. If there is anyone between the two of us who can help him, my money's on you."

"Unfortunately, I have no remedy for a broken heart," Doc replied solemnly.

Katie's shoulders sank when she heard his words. She leaned back against the top rail of the steps.

"He knows about King?"

"He does."

"What did he say when you told him?"

"I didn't tell him."

"I don't understand. Then how did he find out?"

Doc just sat there staring into the distance, slowly rocking, the curved legs of the chair easing over warped floorboards.

"Doc?"

He set his coffee down on the small table next to him and clasped his hands together on his lap. "I wish I had all the answers right now—I really do. But, I don't," he said, looking away. "You should try and get some more rest, it's still early."

"I don't need any more rest. You've been telling me nothing but to rest for almost two days. I need to know that Kyle is okay."

"Kyle will be fine. In time."

"How can you be so calm about all of this?"

Doc stood up and started to walk back inside. "Join me for an early breakfast, then?" he asked.

"How can you just ignore Kyle like this, and go on about your day as if nothing happened?" Katie's patience was quickly turning to anger.

"I think I have a few eggs left if you'd like."

"You can abandon Kyle if you want to, but I won't," Katie said as she stomped down the steps and away from the house.

31

KATIE RAN ACROSS THE DIRT TRACKS in front of the house and into what was left of the barn. For a moment she had forgotten about the fire, but as she stood in the middle of the ruined structure she let out a hushed gasp.

The once-faded red boards were black, stained with the ash of burned wood. The far right side of the barn, where the loft used to be, no longer existed, and the roof on the left side cantilevered precariously over what remained of the dog pens.

Katie stepped through piles of splintered wood and noticed leashes, rigging, and other various tools mixed in. Some of them were burned so badly they were barely recognizable, while others were seemingly untouched. The smell of burned wood, plastic, and steel were heavy in the air around her as she walked.

She made her way through the pens until she found an overturned table. It was the same table she had seen a couple of days earlier, when she'd first discovered the loft. It was only big enough for one person to sit at, and housed two drawers on the right side. She lifted it up and turned it back on all fours, as if that small gesture might mean something to this old barn. One of the drawers was jarred open. When she bent to shut it, she noticed something inside.

She pried the drawer open with her fingers and nearly ripped it off the tracks, stumbling backward a few steps. Regaining her balance, she looked down to find the same brown book she had seen before. It seemed mostly unharmed by the fire. She picked it up and held it in front of her with two hands, almost as if she were reading a map.

Katie folded the cover back on itself and rested against the desk as she flipped through the book.

There was an assortment of poems, and quotes, and passages. Most of them from famous writers that she recognized. Her fingers continued delicately across the pages until she found words she must have read a thousand times. Words that she had heard Doc speak. Words her father wrote.

She took a deep breath, fighting back the well of emotions and closed the book, pushing it back into the drawer.

Katie took another deep breath as she looked around the barn once more. Closing her eyes, she calmed herself.

I need to find Kyle.

Then, she heard a familiar rumble in the distance. She walked outside the barn, or what was left of it, until she had a clear view to the south. A gray sky was quickly turning black, blotting out the late morning light. A flash of white flickered far in the distance. A storm was coming.

And that meant she knew exactly where Kyle would be.

32

KATIE APPROACHED using the same path Kyle had shown her. When she turned the last corner down the dirt path, she expected to see him sitting underneath the large oak tree. She could picture him with his back against the thick base, his legs outstretched. Just looking out to the fields. Watching.

But as she approached, she didn't see anyone. She walked a complete circle around the tree and then out into the field, looking as far as she could see in every direction. He wasn't there.

He has to be here.

Katie's mind began to race again, but she stopped herself, Kyle's words echoing in the back of her mind.

The dogs see everything. The way you walk, the lightness or heaviness of a single step. The way you look at things, with curiosity or insecurity. Even the way you breathe. They take the time to notice the details that we often take for granted.

Katie bent to one knee and placed her hand over the cool grass as she breathed in deep and exhaled slowly, calming herself. She shook her body as chills ran from her shoulders and down her back.

Being around Kyle had changed her. She felt more intuitive, more aware.

She looked around again—at the large angel oak behind her, stretching its limbs like an old man reaching for a memory. The tulip poplars showing more yellow than a week ago. And the sourwoods, sweetgums, and dogwoods turning deep red, while the larger hardwoods had subtler changes. She could even smell the crisp autumn leaves as they fell softly amongst the blades of Carolina bluegrass that stretched down to the foothills from the distant Blue Ridge Mountains.

Her eyes settled on the tall, thin grass that poked up between her fingers, still pressed against the ground. She looked closer, the individual blades shivering at each gust of wind. Her mind hadn't processed it yet, but she had been staring right at it for several seconds. One solitary boot print. And then another. And another.

The girl who had left California two weeks ago would have never noticed any of this. But that same girl now stood in the lowlands of South Carolina following a pair of boot prints for several feet, until she realized where they led.

The cottage.

33

KYLE SAT ON THE BENCH SWING that hung from a tree limb in front of the house. He favored one side, resting his elbow on the wooden armrest, which caused the swing to hang uneven. He stared up towards the light blue sky.

He didn't even move as Katie approached, and she wondered how long he had been sitting here. The bandage across his forehead was gone, and in its place was a jagged cut several inches long. She thought she saw his jeans bunch up where several more bandages on his legs might be.

Katie sat down next to him. Chips of brittle white paint crumbled beneath her from all the weathered years of disuse.

Kyle didn't take his eyes off the morning sky, even as the chains groaned at the added weight. The stars were still visible in the distance, a pale white compared to the sun, trying to hold on just a little longer.

At first Katie just sat next to him quietly. Several minutes of silence passed, though the time felt longer than her entire stay. The time dragged on, until finally Katie's heart overflowed with two simple words.

"I'm sorry."

Kyle didn't respond. He didn't even acknowledge her presence. He just continued looking out into the distance. Away from the farm. Away from her.

Katie thought about just leaving him alone. The cottage was right here. She could go sit inside and wait until he was ready to talk. Maybe it was too soon. Maybe she'd made a mistake trying to find him. But the more she thought about it, the more it didn't make any sense. Why would he come here? There were thousands of acres he could get lost in. But he was here.

Kyle stood up and took several steps forward, leaving Katie to sway uncomfortably on the bench alone.

She watched him as he stood staring into the morning sky. His hands dipped into the crest of his front pockets and his weight leaned to the right. His white and navy trucker hat was pulled down tight over his eyes. The way he looked reminded Katie of the first night she had seen him—guarded.

She dragged her feet lightly on the ground until the bench came to a stop, then stood. She took several steps, until she was next to Kyle. Without realizing it, she extended her hand and lay it on his shoulder.

Kyle's touch was unexpected as he reached up and covered her hand with his own. She could feel the calluses that lined his palms as they slid across the back of her hand. Katie stood with him for a moment. Then, Kyle exhaled a deep breath and wrapped his hand around hers, lifting it off his shoulder. She thought back to that day in the barn.

She waited for him to push her away, but he didn't let go. Instead, he held her hand out in front of him like the beginning of a waltz. As they faced each other, he didn't avoid her gaze.

But as Katie looked back, all she felt was guilt, and it welled up in her like a wave ready to crash on the beach at any moment. And then, it crashed.

She stepped forward, burying her head in his chest. "I'm sorry, Kyle. I'm so sorry." Tears streamed down her cheeks as her body began to tremble.

Then, there was warmth—like stepping out of a shadow on a cool autumn day. His hands pulled her tighter against him as he wrapped his arms around her. She slid her own arms around his waist.

They stood there for several minutes before Kyle spoke. His mouth was just above her head, and his words were a gentle hum. "When I was younger, Doc used to always read to me. He'd grab books by Plato, Aristotle, Seneca, Shakespeare, or Thoreau. But no matter what he read, I always wanted to hear more Emerson. To this day I don't think I understand half of what he wrote, but the words themselves just felt powerful. There was this one essay though." Kyle paused, exhaling. "In it, he wrote 'the remembrance of these visions outlasts all other visions.'"

Katie stepped back and looked up towards Kyle, wiping the tears from her eyes. Her father had loved Emerson—she knew the verse well. It was a beautiful line, full of love and hope. But when Kyle spoke the words all she felt was pain.

He lifted his cap and ran his fingers through his hair as he let out a deep breath. "I've been trying all morning to just remember King, but it's like my vision of him is already fading. It means…Emerson was wrong."

She wanted so badly to tell him that everything would be all right, but she knew those simple words would mean nothing. As she tried to think of words that would carry some meaning, she began to realize she didn't need words at all.

Katie grabbed Kyle by the hand. "Come with me."

She pulled him hard enough that he almost tripped over his own boots. Katie felt him try to resist, but she wouldn't allow it. She had an idea. And she believed it to be a good one.

34

KYLE ALMOST TRIPPED AGAIN as Katie pulled him up the stairs and into the cottage. She let go of his hand and walked over to the dining room table.

Katie watched him look around the room at all her papers, sticky notes, pads, and pictures spread all over the place. She half expected him to start organizing all the piles into nice neat stacks.

Writing isn't a process. It's a mess. That was one of the first things her father taught her. *The sooner you realize this is about to be a disaster, the sooner you can get over it and just write.*

In Katie's mind, it was shaping up to be a beautiful mess. Each pile made up a single scene. There were a little over twenty scenes; eventually, she would piece them all together and then fill in the gaps. For now, though, it was all about just getting it down. Whenever she was in a flow, she'd usually type on her laptop. Random thoughts were scribbled on sticky tabs, and if she was away from her laptop she'd write in her own made-up shorthand on a spiral notepad she always carried. Most of the pictures she'd taken were on her phone, but she kept a portable printer with her, as well. She liked to put a picture on the top of each pile. It helped her visualize the scene.

The dining room table wasn't quite big enough for all her scenes, so she'd moved some to the kitchen counter and some to the couch in the living room just a few feet away.

Katie could feel Kyle's eyes on her as she walked around each pile, picking through them and then tossing them back, like an old lady at a grocery store trying to find the perfect peach.

"Here it is," she said. She walked over to Kyle, who had pulled out a chair at the table and was looking from pile to pile. Most of the pictures were of his dogs. There were Biscuit, Belle, and the pups lying on the porch. Story and Link on their hind legs play fighting, and Olympia and Giza curled up asleep like soft springs.

Then Katie set another photo down in front of Kyle.

* * *

A tightening sensation gripped Kyle's throat. In the photo, Kyle knelt in front of the barn. King was standing on his hind legs, his forepaws resting on Kyle's shoulders. His mouth was closed and his ears lay flat against his head as he stared down at Kyle.

Kyle pressed his fingers against the picture as Katie watched. "I asked Doc why you did that once," Katie said.

"Did what?" Kyle said, not even looking up from the image in his hands.

"Doc said you called it 'hand over heart'?"

Kyle let out a deep breath. He didn't want to explain how aggressive King had been towards other dogs—and people—when Kyle raised him; how he had killed a coyote that approached the barn one evening, and had bitten Doc on several occasions.

"It was the only way I knew to calm the dogs."

Katie seemed to consider his answer, pacing several steps around the kitchen. He knew she had more questions—she always did. They rolled off her tongue like a jumble of words that she just had to say or she might forget. "How exactly does it work? In the field that one day, I saw you whisper something to each of the dogs, right?"

The scraping sound of wood against wood echoed lightly around the dining room as Kyle pushed the chair back from the table and stood. He walked over towards Katie, leaning against the kitchen counter. She straightened nervously as he stood in front of her.

For the second time that day, his hand reached for hers. Katie took several small steps backward until she bumped into the kitchen counter.

His eyes moved from her eyes to her hand as he placed her palm on the left side of his chest. He covered her hand with his and pressed it against his chest, holding it there until she could feel the slow rhythm of his heart.

"Doctors used to check the heart by simply putting an ear on the patient's chest. They would listen for two distinct sounds, a 'lub,' followed by a 'dub.'"

Kyle tapped his fingers over Katie's hand for several beats, her soft skin brushing against his. .

"That was about as scientific a term as you'd get a couple hundred years ago. But make no mistake, they knew what to listen for. The 'lub' is the sound of the first set of heart valves closing. The 'dub' is the sound of the second set closing. "

Kyle pressed slightly on Katie's hand again. "Most doctors would listen for both beats, or for irregularities in those beats. But it's not the beat of the heart that is most important. It's the quiet between the beats."

"What if it's not quiet?" Katie asked.

"Well, it could mean a lot of things. There could be a heart murmur, which often sounds like a 'whoosh.' Or there could be signs of heart failure. Really, any irregularity can indicate a problem."

"But you're not listening to the dog's heart," Katie said.

"You're right. Doc is the doctor, not me."

"I don't get it, then."

"I'm not listening to the heart. I'm looking for a way in. If the eyes are the window to the soul, then the heart is the front door. I'm just reminding the dog that amongst everything, there is a quiet within."

Kyle let go of Katie's hand and walked back over towards the table. Towards the pictures of his dogs. It felt different to see them from her point of view. It was like looking at them from the side instead of head on. But it was a side he was grateful to see.

Before Katie could step away from the counter, Kyle turned back towards her, closing the space between them again.

He took off his hat, leaned in, and kissed Katie on the cheek.

As he pulled away he wanted to say so much. *Thank you for being honest. Thank you for helping Belle. Thank you for the pictures, and this moment I will never forget.*

Instead, he just said, "thank you," and walked away.

* * *

The sound of the front door closing pulled Katie from her trance. Why did he have to kiss her like that? His lips had been warm and soft, in direct contrast to the five o'clock shadow that chafed her soft skin as it brushed against her. This wasn't supposed to be complicated. She was here to write a story. Nothing more.

She pressed her hand over the spot on her cheek where his lips had been. The longer she stood there, the more she began to realize that she wanted more than a story. She rushed out, ready to jog down the front steps after Kyle, but when she swung the door open there was no reason to run. Kyle stood in front of her, waiting.

She caught her breath as they stood facing one another. She felt like she needed to say something. Anything. But no words came out. For a moment, she was back on her porch in California staring at a blinking cursor and a blank screen. She was lost.

Until his lips found hers for the first time.

Kyle moved slow and sure, as if he had planned out every step he would make to cover the seven feet of space between them. His hand reached her face and slid behind the cusp of her neck and into her hair as he subtly tilted her head back and pressed his lips to hers.

Then, he pulled back for a moment as he leaned his forehead against hers.

Katie opened her eyes and looked up towards Kyle. She knew he was thinking out the situation, trying to plan out every detail. But she also knew this was not something he could have planned for. It was nothing more than a simple choice—yes, or no.

She watched his eyes, and for a moment she thought he might back away. Her heart sank at the thought of him leaving her again. Then she felt his hand tighten slightly on her neck as he pulled her closer.

The Katie who had first come here wouldn't have been able to hold back the questions filling every corner of her mind. She would have been consumed by the not knowing.

His hands moved to her waist and then lower. She sighed into his mouth as he lifted her up. She wrapped her legs around him as he backed her against the front door. The warmth of his lips felt good against hers.

Kyle pushed the door open and as he stepped through the threshold she realized the Katie who had first come here was gone.

She realized he'd chosen yes.

35

KYLE WOKE TO A COOL GUST of late-autumn wind that swept through the open bedroom window, causing the sheer curtains to rise and fall like a quiet tide. He turned his head on the pillow to find Katie curled up next to him. The lower half of her body was pressed up against him, their feet tangled together like two people who had succumbed to the comfort of sleep but weren't willing to part.

He pulled the sheets back quietly, revealing the subtle outline of her body. He loved the way his hands felt around the soft skin where the small of her back ran into her waist. She was slender, yet strong and graceful.

When he slid out of bed he realized his body felt more relaxed than it had in a long time. He locked his hands together behind his back and stretched his shoulders, then twisted from side to side. It took a few seconds for his mind to catch up to his eyes, but as he walked over to shut the window he saw nothing but darkness and the white light of the same stars from this morning. They'd been in the cottage—barely leaving this bedroom—for an entire afternoon, and late into the night.

Another breeze entered through an open window in the kitchen and lifted several pieces of paper off the table and onto the floor. Kyle left Katie to sleep and walked over to pick them up. They were more pictures.

He sat down at the table and stacked the pictures neatly in front of him. His fingers found the corners of each photo, pushing them around slightly until he couldn't tell it was a stack of three photos, but appeared to be just one. The picture on top wasn't of any of the dogs, but rather him. He was kneeling below the angel oak at Old Man's Crossing. The picture was taken from behind him, looking out towards an oncoming storm. Kyle remembered the day well—it was the day he'd taken Katie to watch King run. He couldn't see King in the distance, but he knew he was out there. Somewhere.

Kyle stood up and walked towards the darkness that lingered just outside the window. It was a beautiful night. The moon hung in a low crescent as the stars played catch with a ball of light. One twinkling, and then another.

From where he stood, the window reflected an image of the room behind him—the same stacks of paper and pictures that he had seen earlier this morning.

He walked over to the table in front of the couch and picked up a stack of hand written pages. He paused for a moment, thinking that reading the words might be some type of intrusion of Katie's world. She had shown him the pictures earlier with no reservation, though. So, he held the paper in front of him and read.

> *You may give them your love but not your thoughts,*
> *For they have their own thoughts.*
> *You may house their bodies but not their souls,*
> *For their souls dwell in the house of tomorrow,*

which you cannot visit, not even in your dreams.
You may strive to be like them,
but seek not to make them like you.
For life goes not backward nor tarries with yesterday.

These weren't Katie's words at all. They were from a famous poem called "The Prophet." Another reading assignment Doc had given him when he was younger.

There were several empty lines below the poem, then more words were written. This time, they were Katie's.

> *Hope is a very strange thing. To always be fleeting and yet to always be near. To be grasped for a moment, but to fade away as if it never existed. Khalil Gibran once wrote, "you can give them your love, but not your thoughts." But more accurately, you can give someone love, but you cannot give them hope. As I watch Kyle with the dogs, I see so much hope in him. The dogs seem to complete him, but still there is something missing.*

> *Now I sit before Kyle as he sleeps, and I'm worried about what will come when he wakes. In life it is difficult to lose your best friend. But when Kyle wakes to find King gone, will he have lost his only friend? I cannot give him my hope. And my deepest fear is that he will find none.*

Kyle set the page down in front of him and looked back towards the room where Katie was sleeping.

I cannot give him my hope.

Was that what she thought he was doing here? Was that why… He stopped, anger and resentment tightening in his chest.

Kyle looked down at the page again. Then, he turned and left.

36

KATIE WOKE TO THE GENTLE groans of the windowpanes expanding under the heat of the morning sun. She smiled before she even opened her eyes, thinking of the day before with Kyle. But as she rolled over and stretched out her arms, she realized he wasn't in bed.

Katie thought of Kyle's morning ritual of walking the fences with King—a ritual she'd only learned of the morning of the fire. Would he be out there now? Alone? It hurt her heart a little to think about it, but she knew this time could also heal him. Maybe he'd even take another of the dogs with him, or even one of the puppies.

She shook off her thoughts as she slipped out of bed, using the rubber band on her wrist to pull back her hair. Her plan for the morning was to write and shower. If she kept the writing to just a couple of hours, then the eggs and bacon that Doc usually made may still be warm by the time she got there. Maybe he'd even make some of his biscuits with peach jam. Katie had learned that even though Georgia might be known as the Peach State, it was South Carolina that had the best peaches.

She tried to focus, though all she could think about now were peaches. She moved from one pile of papers to the next, trying to find some point of inspiration that would set her off in a journey of words. But every pile was another delicious peach. Peach cobbler, peach jam, peach tea, peach pie, peach dump cake. Her stomach growled. She was famished. And as she got up from the table, she realized she was more excited to see Kyle than anything.

* * *

Whenever driving a nail into a hard wood like laurel oak, it's important to take care to prevent the wood from splitting. Kyle knew that some people spent time lubricating the nails with beeswax, but blunting the nail by simply tapping the point with a hammer worked just fine. Avoiding the grain of the wood as a starting point for the nail also helped.

As Kyle nailed the hog wire to the post for the new dog pens that morning, however, he didn't care about any of that. He didn't hold the hammer firmly near the middle like he was shaking hands. He didn't tap the nail lightly until it sank into the wood enough to stand on its own. He hit it once as hard as he could and then a second time to finish it, leaving an imprint of the hammer head in the post.

He was angry. Angry at this stupid piece of hog wire that wouldn't stay taut. Angry at himself for getting involved with a girl from California who was clearly here for nothing more than a story. Even angry at King for dying.

Kyle threw the hammer at the ground. The flat claw end stuck in the dirt like a hatchet. He picked up the shovel and moved to the next post. He should have dug all the post holes first, placed the posts, and then set the wire. But he wasn't thinking clearly. He had no plan—he just worked as he went.

* * *

Katie didn't find Kyle in the house, not that she expected him to be there. To her dismay, she didn't find eggs and bacon, either. But she did find a plate of biscuits and a jar of peach jam with a note that made her laugh.

Don't eat all the biscuits!

Doc

She must have just missed him, because the biscuits were still warm when she cut into them. Three biscuits later, she was full.

Katie walked outside and sat down in one of the rocking chairs on the porch. The sun had been up for a little over an hour and typically Kyle was back by now, so she figured he'd be walking up any minute. Normally, she would have been content to just sit on the porch and enjoy the slow cadence of rocking, but the view was no longer the same.

In place of the faded red barn with several oaks and flowered bushes crowding each side, were ash-covered ground and portions of timber walls that stood precariously on edge. So, instead of letting her mind wander to several nights before, she decided she would walk around back. Thanks to the fire, Kyle had been forced to use the runs before they were completed, and she had yet to really look at them.

Katie walked down the porch and along the side of the house. It sat on a cluster of cinderblocks about every ten feet, and halfway in she saw a familiar black and white tail alongside one. She knelt down by Biscuit, who was napping in the crawl space under the house. The dog's tail began to wag and she stood to greet Katie.

"Hey, girl," Katie said as she ran her hand through Biscuit's fur. "Whatcha doin' today?"

Biscuit parted her lips and started panting, which looked like a smile to Katie.

"You wouldn't happen to know where Kyle is, would you?" Biscuit's ears perked at the sound of Kyle's name. Katie stood, still looking down at the black and white dog. Her eyebrows were accented with tan markings that gave her a very inquisitive look. "Well, I'm going to walk around back for a bit if you want to come." Sure enough, Biscuit followed Katie as she walked, the dog trotting several paces behind and to the side of her.

A few seconds later, Katie heard a faint sound.

Shhnnnk.

Then she heard it again.

Shhnnkk.

When she made it past the farthest corner of the house, she saw the nearly finished runs. There were a total of seven. Each run was approximately twenty feet wide and a hundred feet long. The posts were eight feet on center and hog wire enclosed each of them, making them more like large pens than anything else. They were all adjacent to one another in neat rows. Two gates, one about ten feet from the end of each run, connected one to the other.

Pine trees, bales of hay, and even old farm equipment had been left untouched. Katie couldn't discern how Doc had split up the dogs after the fire, but she was sure that Kyle had already moved them around. He was very particular about how the dogs interacted. Some were more dominant, while others were more submissive, and grouping them could mean the difference between two dogs curled up together or two dogs biting at each other.

Katie heard the sound again before she saw Kyle.

Shhnnk.

She looked towards the far end of the last run, opposite where she stood. There, she saw Kyle slam a post-hole digger into the ground and pull out a clump of dirt. And then again. And again.

He didn't look up once as Katie walked towards him. She didn't mind, as it gave her the opportunity to watch him work. His thighs strained beneath tight blue jeans, and the muscles in his upper arm flexed into a small horseshoe as he pushed the shovel into the ground. It was easy for Katie to admit now that the moment she'd first seen him she'd been attracted. As she watched him, she just wanted him to wrap his arms around her. To pull her close to him like the day before. But even when Katie was only a few feet away, Kyle didn't make any motion to turn around and greet her. It was as if she wasn't even there.

"What are you doing?" Katie said.

Kyle stopped momentarily and rested the shovel underneath his chin as he turned to face her. "I was trying to dig out these last few holes to finish the seventh run, but I imagine that's probably just hopeless," he said, his emphasis on the last word.

Katie's smile faded. "Why do you say that?"

"Look around. You tell me. The dirt, the dust, the emptiness. What is there to hope for?" Kyle stared intently at Katie. She was reminded of a wounded animal trying to inflict the same pain it felt.

She was caught off guard, but she realized immediately what he was referring to. "You read my work?"

Kyle didn't answer. Instead, he just jammed the shovel back into the earth and continued working.

She wanted to scream at him. He had no right to read her words—even if they were about him. It was still her private thoughts. But her feelings softened as she continued to watch him, his eyes fixed on the ground, his jaw tight as he grit through the pain of what he was trying to do. He was hurt, and in being hurt trying to hurt back.

With the loss of King still a fresh wound, Katie didn't press the issue. She didn't yell or react in the way she knew she was justified. Instead, she explained.

"Those were unfinished words, just thoughts on a page. They don't mean what you think."

"And what exactly do I think they mean?" Kyle offered as bait.

Katie didn't bite. "Kyle, that's not fair. You know what I'm trying to say. Those words were not meant—"

He cut her off. "—for me to read?" He shook his head as he continued to stare at the ground. Then he looked up at her, holding her gaze. "You were right. I am hopeless without him. Everything about me felt empty when I woke and he was gone. And then...yesterday happened."

Katie's eyes were wet as she stepped forward, touching Kyle lightly on the shoulder.

He shrugged her off, turning away from her as Biscuit and Belle came padding up behind him, tails wagging. They both rose on their hind legs, resting their forepaws against the chicken wire, peering in at the other dogs. Katie moved forward again with her hand facing the ground, to pet them. Before they could reach her, Kyle harshly corrected them, signing fiercely for them to get down and back away.

Belle ran off, but Biscuit sat next to him, ears pressed flat against her neck, her head hung low. Kyle signaled again, this time also snapping his fingers and Biscuit trotted off, looking back several times.

"Why did you do that? Just because you're mad at me doesn't mean you have to treat them like that."

"Mad at you?" Kyle scoffed. "I'm not mad at you. I'm disappointed."

Katie's heart sank when she heard those words. They struck her like lightning.

"I understand how you see me—some lost boy hanging on to a bunch of dogs like a child because it's the only thing I know. And maybe you're right. I've hardly even left this farm since my parents died."

"What do you want from me?" she asked.

Kyle glanced at Katie, tears streaming from her eyes, and then turned his back on her. He picked up the shovel. "I want you to go."

She had no words. She just stood there for a moment, motionless. Her eyes moved from Kyle to the dogs. The only thing she noticed before she walked away was the absence of King.

37

IT TOOK KATIE LESS than an hour to get all her things together, and almost another hour to lug them from the cottage to her car.

It had only been ten days, but it felt weird to open the door to her car. The light blue metal was caked in a layer of beige dust and bits of clay.

She walked back to the house thinking she'd leave Doc a quick thank-you note, but when she got to the steps he was waiting for her.

"Leaving so soon?" Doc said.

Katie tried to force a smile. "I think I have officially worn out my welcome."

"Nonsense. You are welcome here anytime and for as long as you'd like."

Not everyone would agree, Katie thought.

"Well, if you really must go, at least let me send you off with a little something. Just give me one second."

"You don't need to…" Katie started to say, but Doc disappeared into the house. When he came back out he was holding a plate of biscuits in one hand and a jar of peach jam in the other.

"Dooocc," Katie whined. "Are you trying to make me fat?"

He handed them to her. "Oh hush, this stuff is good for you. It's got peaches in it."

Katie stopped laughing for a moment and looked at Doc seriously. "Doc. I really do appreciate you letting me stay for so long."

"Like I said before—you are welcome here anytime. Anytime at all."

"May I ask one more favor?"

"Anything."

She opened her purse and pulled out a brown canvas book with gold lettering etched across the cover. There was a folded piece of paper stuck in between the pages. She handed the book to Doc and said, "Would you give this to Kyle?"

Doc nodded. "Of course."

Katie turned and took several steps down the porch stairs and then paused at the bottom. "By the way—the painting you have? I looked it up. It means 'Fall seven times; stand up eight.'"

Doc smiled. "Yes, Miss Price. I know."

"But I thought you said you didn't know what it meant."

"Did I? I s'pose sometimes the things we say aren't always the things we mean."

And with that he walked back into the house, letting the makeshift screen door clatter behind him one last time.

38

Dear Kyle,

Letters often remind me of pictures. There is always so much you want to capture, but only so much you are able to. With that in mind, most of what I want to say is just thank you.

Thank you for letting me walk into your world as a stranger and leave as a friend, even if you would not consider us that any longer.

Thank you for allowing me time with the dogs, time that I will treasure forever.

Thank you for hoping that night in the barn when all hope may have been lost. I owe you my life, a life I would gladly trade to give you King's back.

Above all I want you to know one last thing. The words that you read on those sheets of paper hurt you. I know this, because they hurt me to write them. But my father always taught me that sometimes the most beautiful stories can only be found in places where we risk everything. Where we are vulnerable and sometimes hopeless.

When I was a little girl, I would beg my father to read me his poems. One of my favorites was in the first book of poems he ever wrote. I loved it so much that one day he tore part of the poem right out of the book for me. I've carried it around for almost fifteen years, and I want you to have it.

> *Let the rain add to our tears*
> *Until the day when all pain has stopped*
> *And we will say there was hope in every raindrop*

Last but not least, please take care of this book. The author's name on the spine is faded. But if you could read it, it would say Matthew Price. My father.

Kyle's hands trembled as he held the torn sheet of paper in his hand. He thumbed through the book until he found the page it had been torn from. Fitting it back to the page he read the poem in full. He must have read it a thousand times as a boy. It had meant so much to him. But now…

He folded the letter back into thirds and turned back towards the house. Doc was standing on the porch, his rocking chair abandoned.

"Did you know?" Kyle asked. Doc didn't respond. "The words you said to me as a boy—those were her father's words. How is that even possible?"

"Have you learned nothing from King?"

Those words struck a painful cord as Kyle lowered his head, and Doc handed over the book. Kyle flipped the pages until he found the poem. "Hope in Every Raindrop." He read it in full, for the first time.

"All things are possible," Doc continued.

Thunder lashed out against the darkened sky. Kyle's chest rose and fell as he breathed heavily. He could almost envision King standing against the horizon as Doc went on.

"There has to be hope. Not because it already exists within you, but because it must exist, period. There is no option to lay down because you're feeling hurt. There is no alternative. It is not live or die. It is live or live. Not because you want it that way, or because you've willed it that way. But because it must be that way.

"King understood this that night in the barn. Now, I'm asking you to understand. You once told me that King would stand out there on rainy days. And just before the rain would fall, he would run. Not from the rain, but before it. As a boy, you'd go on and on about it.

"But you were wrong. He did not run from the rain, or before it. He ran to you. And now you have to run to her."

Doc didn't even finish his words before Kyle handed him the book and took off.

"I didn't actually mean to literally run after her," Doc yelled. But the sound of screeching tires and a horn drowned out his words.

39

KATIE PULLED TO THE EDGE of the property where the dirt road ended and the paved road began. She looked to her right, down the same road that had led her here. She didn't want to leave. She didn't want to leave the dogs and Doc. She didn't want to leave Kyle. Why couldn't he understand they were just words on a page? *Why does he look past me and see the words? Why can't he look past the words and see me?*

Katie leaned her head forward against the steering wheel as small drops of rain began to fall against her windshield.

She watched the rain dance across her window and listened to the thunder echo over the land. Something about it calmed her. She took a deep breath, and sat back up.

For a moment, she thought about turning around and trying to explain everything to him one more time. But she knew it wouldn't work.

Katie lifted her foot off the brake and turned the steering wheel to the right. Her front tires crunched over the dirt road and onto the wet asphalt. She looked to the left, back to the right, and then slammed on her brakes.

A truck laid on its horn and swerved around her as it came around the corner, but she didn't even blink. Standing in front of her was a large black dog. It wasn't just any black dog, though. Its front legs were lean and narrow. Its chest broad, and its eyes fixed on Katie. It was King.

Katie put the car in park and swung open the door. The dog didn't move.

The rain sounded like tiny drummers against the canvas top of her car. She opened the door and stepped out. The dog didn't move.

She took several steps, then stopped.

How is this possible? This isn't possible.

"King?" she said, almost silently.

The dog looked to the right, and Katie followed its gaze behind her.

That's when she saw him.

He was several hundred feet from her, but she knew it was him. Every movement he made seemed to have a specific purpose. He turned slightly to the left just before he approached a small dip in the road, and then back right to avoid a large rock. He was moving at such a furious pace. He was moving like King.

She turned back around and the dog was gone. Katie ran out into the road where the dog was standing and looked all around. Nothing.

"Katie!" Kyle yelled from about fifty feet away.

She froze.

Kyle continued running until he was about ten feet away, and then stopped.

She could see his chest rise and fall, his breathing heavy, as he walked towards her. She didn't move. It felt like every muscle in her body had contracted, and she struggled to catch her breath.

When he was just a foot away he stopped. "Hi," he said.

"Hi," she returned.

Kyle reached down for her hand, his touch surprising her. For a moment he didn't say anything. He just looked down as he ran his thumb over her fingers.

"So...what brings you all the way out here?" Katie said, smiling awkwardly.

Kyle didn't smile with her. He didn't respond to her comment. He lifted his eyes towards hers and said the only two words she wanted to hear: "Don't leave."

"I'm sorry," he said. "I didn't mean what I said earlier. I was just..."

"I know," she said.

Kyle didn't know what else to say. She could see it in his eyes. And for that reason, he didn't need to say anything at all. Katie leaned in and kissed him.

Kyle followed her back to her car. The rain was letting up and the dark clouds overhead were moving quickly towards the east.

As she reached the car she said, "I'll stay on one condition." She looked back to where King had been standing. "Tell me more about King."

40

DOC WAS WAITING FOR THEM on the porch when they got back to the house. But as they approached, their clothes still wet from the rain, he didn't say a word.

Kyle carried her bags past Doc and set them in his bedroom against the wall.

"Do you mind if I take a shower?" Katie said.

"Not at all." Kyle pulled off his wet shirt and walked over to the laundry basket on the bed full of clean clothes.

Katie didn't take her eyes off him as he pulled the new shirt over his head.

"What?" Kyle said.

"Oh, nothing," Katie said with a smile.

Kyle walked over and stood in front of Katie. "I've got a few things to finish up with the new pens, so I'll probably be out back." Then he leaned in and surprised her with a kiss. It wasn't a long kiss, or a passionate kiss. It was just a kiss from a guy. The right guy.

When Katie finished her shower she dried her hair the best she could with a towel, and pulled on a pair of jeans and a shirt.

As she stepped through the front door she found Doc still sitting on the porch. The rain was gone and several rays of sun cascaded through the pines. She looked over at him, but he didn't look back up at her.

"Doc?" she said. "Everything okay?"

Without lifting his arm off the chair, he pointed. She looked down to see Kyle kneeling just off the side of the house. He was with one of Biscuit's puppies. The all black one—the same one Katie had been holding that day she first saw King.

Surprisingly, the dog sat still for a moment as Kyle placed his hand over its small chest. Then the little dog squirmed and started to bite at his finger.

Katie couldn't help but smile because she knew that Kyle would find a way into his heart. Just as he'd found a way into hers.

About the Author

Wesley Banks was born and raised in Bradenton, Florida. He graduated from the University of Florida with a Bachelor's and Master's degree in Civil Engineering. After spending over 7 years building movable bridges from Florida to Washington he decided to focus on his true passion: writing.

Wesley recently moved to Oregon to get back to the great outdoors that he loves so much. He lives with his wife Lindsey, and his two dogs Linkin and Story. Most of his time these days is spent writing, with as much rock climbing, hiking, or skiing as he can fit in.

Author Page: WesleyBanksAuthor.com

Note from the Author

I sincerely hope you have enjoyed reading this book as much as I enjoyed writing it.

If so, I would love for you to do two things:

1. Leave a review telling what you loved about the book.
2. Come find me at <u>WesleyBanksAuthor.com</u> and let's connect. I love catching up with my readers.

Made in the USA
Lexington, KY
18 June 2015